Diseases and Disorders of Youth

Kids and Asthma

Kris Hirschmann

ReferencePoint Press®

San Diego, CA

ReferencePoint Press®

Printed in the United States

For more information, contact:
ReferencePoint Press, Inc.
PO Box 27779
San Diego, CA 92198
www.ReferencePointPress.com

LIBRARY OF CONGRESS CATALOGING-IN-PUBLICATION DATA

Name: Hirschmann, Kris, author.
Title: Kids and Asthma/by Kris Hirschmann.
Description: San Diego, CA: ReferencePoint Press, Inc., 2019. | Series: Diseases and Disorders of Youth | Audience: Grade 9 to 12. | Includes bibliographical references and index.
Identifiers: LCCN 2018011690 (print) | LCCN 2018011762 (ebook) | ISBN 9781682823941 (eBook) | ISBN 9781682823934 (hardback)
Subjects: LCSH: Asthma in children—Juvenile literature. | Asthmatics—Juvenile literature. | Asthma in children—Treatment—Juvenile literature. | Asthma in children—Prevention—Juvenile literature. | Asthma—Miscellanea.
Classification: LCC RJ436.A8 (ebook) | LCC RJ436.A8 H57 20196 (print) | DDC 618.92/238—dc23
LC record available at https://lccn.loc.gov/2018011690

Contents

Introduction

The Most Common Chronic Disease of Youth

Neel Duggal clearly remembers the day his health took a turn for the worse. Eight years old at the time, Duggal was running sprints up and down a field with his soccer team of three years. This particular day was cold and windy, and suddenly, Duggal recalls, "I started coughing. I thought I was coming down with a cold at first. I could tell that something was different about this, though. I felt like there was liquid in my lungs. No matter how deeply I inhaled, I couldn't catch my breath. Before I knew it, I was wheezing uncontrollably."[1]

The moment passed, and Duggal shrugged it off. As the weeks passed, though, Duggal found himself coughing more frequently and violently during practice. He eventually had a coughing fit so severe that he had to be taken to the emergency room. There, he says, "a doctor asked me a lot of questions about my breathing . . . what symptoms I had and when they were worse. After taking in the information, he told me I might have asthma."[2]

Duggal's story is far from unique. Around the world thousands of children are diagnosed with asthma every day. This chronic disease is characterized by recurrent attacks of breathlessness, wheezing, and sometimes coughing, which vary in severity and frequency from person to person. It is the most common chronic disease among children worldwide.

A Global Problem

A look at the numbers shows just how widespread asthma is. In the United States alone, the Centers for Disease Control and Prevention (CDC) reports that 8.4 percent of all children aged eighteen and under have asthma. This equals about 6.2 million individuals. Including adults in the number brings the total to nearly 25 million. Globally, the numbers are staggering. The World Health Organization reports that in 2015, the most recent year for which numbers are available, about 235 million people, both children and adults, suffered from asthma. Other organizations believe that the number is even higher, with estimates of up to 330 million asthma sufferers worldwide.

> **"No matter how deeply I inhaled, I couldn't catch my breath. Before I knew it, I was wheezing uncontrollably."[1]**
>
> —Neel Duggal, asthma sufferer

In the United States, 2017 CDC statistics reveal some interesting trends among people with asthma. The disorder is most common among African American children, with 13.4 percent receiving an asthma diagnosis. The figure falls to 8 percent among Hispanic children and 7.4 percent among white children. Children of all other ethnicities combined have an asthma rate of 8.4 percent. In all ethnicities, asthma strikes females more often than males—for every two boys who receive an asthma diagnosis, about three girls will develop this disorder.

On the Rise

The numbers were probably not always this high. Although statistics are not available for the early through mid-1900s, asthma did not become a serious public health concern until 1977, when a rash of asthma-related deaths rocked the world medical community. Around the same time, hospital admissions for asthma started to rise dramatically in most developed countries, including New Zealand, Australia, the United Kingdom, Canada, and the United States.

Based on this information, scientists at first believed that asthma was rising only in high-income countries. But in 1991 an initiative called the International Study of Asthma and Allergies in Childhood (ISAAC) proved this assumption wrong. This twenty-year program monitored asthma and allergies in ninety-eight countries around the world. Its data show clearly that childhood asthma is a common disease nearly everywhere, regardless of a region's income or development status.

ISAAC's data show another interesting trend. It appears that in developed countries, the incidence of childhood asthma started to level out in the early 2000s. In developing countries, however, particularly those with large populations, the incidence of asthma has continued to rise. These areas are quickly catching up to the developed world. It remains to be seen whether asthma rates in low-income countries will continue to rise or will level off, as they have in higher-income areas.

Why Does It Matter?

In the developed world, nearly everyone knows someone with asthma. Asthmatic people may wheeze and cough from time to time. Perhaps they have to sit out a few sports games or take some medicine. It may not seem like such a big deal.

Asthma Prevalence in the United States

The most recent available data from the Centers for Disease Control and Prevention breaks down the incidence of asthma in American children by age, sex, and race. Data from 2015 shows that asthma occurs more often in children than adults and more often in girls than boys. It is most common among black individuals and least common among those of Hispanic descent.

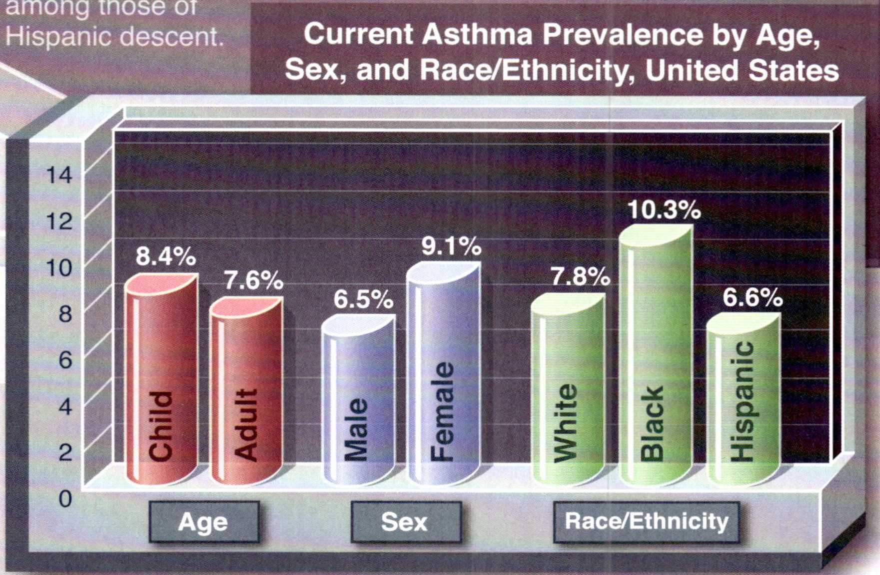

Source: Centers for Disease Control and Prevention, "Asthma Surveillance Data," September 2016. www.cdc.gov.

Uncontrolled asthma, however, is a very big deal indeed. Around the world, the World Health Organization estimates that 383,000 people die each year as a result of asthma. In the United States asthma killed 3,615 people in 2015; of these deaths, 219 were children aged eighteen or younger. Many other sufferers needed significant medical attention. The CDC reports that in the United States asthma causes about 2 million emergency room visits each year. Health care costs for these cases and other asthma-related hospital visits total at least $56 billion and perhaps over $80 billion annually, according to various estimates.

Considering that the United States accounts for just 4.4 percent of earth's population, the worldwide total may be twenty times higher or even more.

To reduce this burden, the World Health Organization is spearheading global efforts to prevent and control asthma. Its objectives are to track asthma data, educate people about how to avoid environmental factors that contribute to asthma, and improve access to medicines and medical care. By doing these things, officials hope to improve the outlook for asthmatic youth and adults alike—particularly in the area of mortality. One recent study found that nearly half of all asthma-related deaths could have been prevented. These results, say scientist Martyn R. Partridge, "should unequivocally lead to a shake-up, more training and monitoring, and an end to the complacency that has arisen regarding this common condition."[3] With attention and further research, there is every hope of improving the outlook for youth with asthma.

Chapter 1

What Is Asthma?

Children who suffer from various disorders do not always have the language to correctly describe their symptoms, and asthma is no exception. On an Internet message board, parents describe some of the things they hear from their young children. "My daughter is five years and she'll say her head hurts . . . or she says she can't breathe or her 'belly hurts' (she holds her chest when she says it so I assume that it is chest tightening that she is confusing as belly pain),"[4] one mother reports.

"My three-year-old says his breathing is stuck,"[5] another mother says. Says yet another mother:

> TJ, who is three years old, won't say anything, he will scratch at his neck and chest. Sometimes he has petechiae (little red dots) on his chest before he even has any other symptoms. He will also tell me he is "cwammy" (he gets clammy when he is too active) and needs his "binger hugger or haler" (pulse [oxygen meter], we call it a finger hugger, and haler is his inhaler [a device that delivers medicine directly to the lungs]). He also gets very short of breath.[6]

All of these children are struggling, with their limited language skills, to put the same thing into words. They are suffering from the uncomfortable symptoms of asthma, a respiratory disease that makes breathing difficult. Asthma affects children of all ages, from infancy onward, and usually persists into adulthood. It is the most common chronic disorder of youth worldwide. In a medical context, the word *chronic* means that a disorder is persistent and not easily cured, if at all. Once it sets in, it tends to affect the individual for life. Asthma falls into this category. If a person experiences the symptoms of asthma even once, it is likely that he or she will be asthmatic to some degree forever.

Asthma Symptoms

The main symptoms of asthma are related to a person's breathing. A child with asthma may have trouble pulling air into the lungs, blowing it back out, or both. This leads to a feeling of being short of breath. "It's kind of like you're trying to breathe through something really small, like through a straw or something," says Susan, a young woman with asthma. "It feels like there's something stopping you kind of breathing properly, like opening and closing your lungs."[7]

> **"It's kind of like you're trying to breathe through something really small, like through a straw or something."[7]**
>
> —Susan, asthma sufferer

Wheezing is another common asthma symptom. Wheezing is a rattling or high-pitched whistling sound made by the airways during breathing. It is caused by air rushing through narrowed or phlegm-filled air passageways. Depending on how badly the airways are affected, wheezing can be loud enough for someone nearby to hear clearly or so subtle that it can be detected only by a doctor with a stethoscope.

Chest tightness, pain, and pressure often accompany these breathing symptoms. "It's like somebody's sitting on your chest and they've got their hands round your throat . . . no matter how hard you breathe in your chest wall feels like it's not moving, at all,"[8] says Catherine, a woman who experienced this symptom.

Coughing is the fourth primary symptom of asthma. Asthmatics of all ages may have a chronic cough that gets worse and better over time but never quite goes away. The cough is often most severe at night or whenever the person lies down. Sitting up relieves the cough but disrupts sleep, which can lead to a constant state of exhaustion. This in turn can lead to anxiety, difficulties with concentration, and other symptoms that interfere with daily life.

How Normal Lungs Work

Asthma is a disorder of the respiratory system and particularly of the lungs. The lungs are organs that absorb oxygen from the air and release carbon dioxide gas from the body. This exchange is vitally important to life. Oxygen is a gas that fuels the cells and helps them produce energy. Carbon dioxide is a waste product

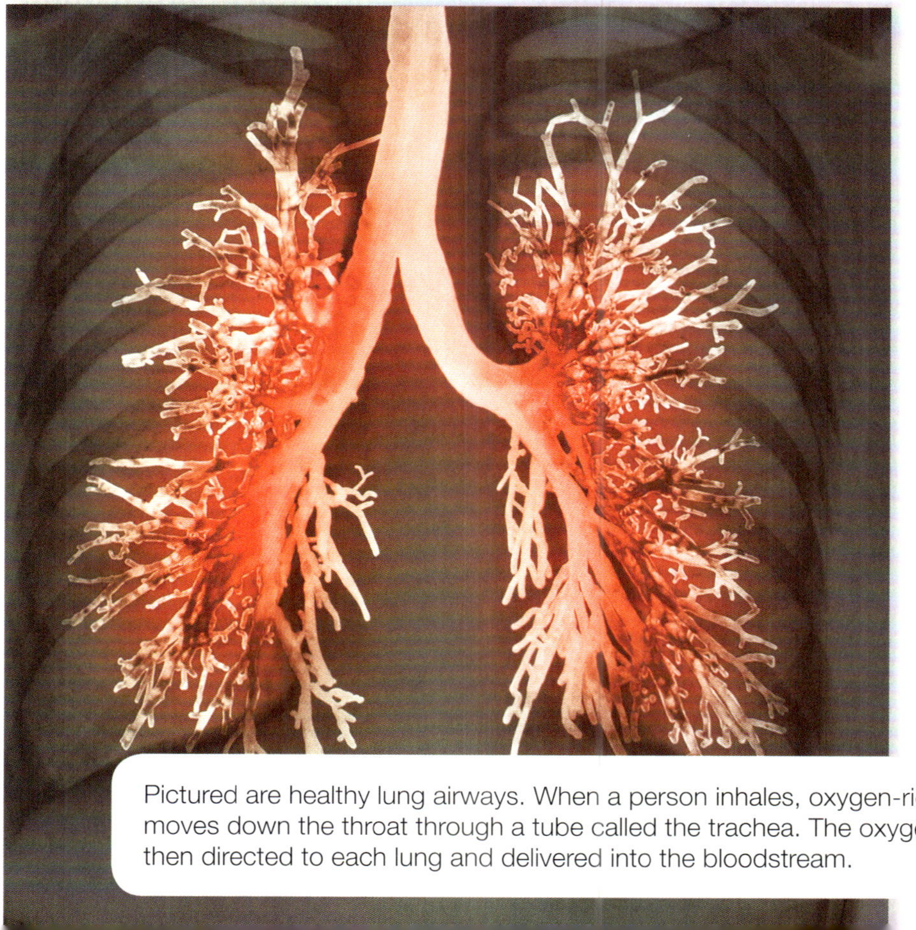

Pictured are healthy lung airways. When a person inhales, oxygen-rich air moves down the throat through a tube called the trachea. The oxygen is then directed to each lung and delivered into the bloodstream.

produced by the cells that, in large amounts, can poison the body. To stay alive, the body must receive a constant new supply of oxygen while removing excess carbon dioxide.

The lungs initiate this process by collecting air whenever a person breathes it in through the mouth, nose, or both. The oxygen-rich air passes down the throat, through a tube called

Asthma Imposters

A person with shortness of breath, wheezing, chest tightness, and coughing may seem to have asthma—but this is not always the case. Many conditions have similar symptoms. When presented with apparent asthma cases, doctors must be careful to rule out these copycat conditions.

sinusitis: Also called a sinus infection, sinusitis can lead to airway constriction, which produces the symptoms of asthma.

myocardial ischemia: This condition is characterized by reduced blood flow to the heart. It often causes shortness of breath.

gastroesophageal reflux disease (GERD): In this disorder, stomach contents flow back into the esophagus, which is the tube that passes food into the stomach. GERD causes chronic heartburn, which can lead to asthma symptoms.

chronic obstructive pulmonary disease (COPD): This is a general term for several lung diseases, often caused by smoking, that have asthma-like symptoms.

congestive heart failure: In this disease the heart does not pump properly, leading to a fluid buildup in the lungs. This buildup impairs the lungs' function and causes breathing problems.

fungal infection: The aspergillus fungus can infect the lungs and cause coughing, wheezing, and shortness of breath.

Some of these copycat disorders, such as COPD and congestive heart failure, are rare in children. Others, such as sinusitis, are quite common. A careful medical examination and testing, if needed, can help determine if a child's symptoms are caused by asthma or by a different problem.

the trachea. Where the trachea meets the lungs, it branches into two smaller tubes called the right and left bronchi, one leading to each lung. The air passes through the bronchi into smaller tubes called bronchioles, which branch off into even smaller tubes called alveolar ducts. These tiny tubes carry air into sacs called alveoli.

The alveoli are like miniature balloons with very thin skin. They are webbed on the outside with tiny blood vessels called capillaries. Blood flows through the capillaries constantly. As it does, carbon dioxide passes from the blood into the alveoli. At the same time, oxygen passes from the alveoli into the blood. This exchange goes on constantly. With each inhaled breath, a person sucks in a new load of oxygen to help fuel the body. With each exhaled breath, he or she releases the blood's poisonous carbon dioxide load.

In a healthy respiratory system, breathing is easy and relaxed. All of the tubes, even the tiny ones, are big enough for air to pass comfortably in and out. A person can feel the breathing process if he or she thinks about it, but most of the time it is unconscious. The body runs the system automatically, and breathing just happens.

Asthmatic Lungs

The situation is entirely different in lungs affected by asthma. People with asthma have very sensitive airways. If any irritants enter the system, the airways react strongly, in the same way a person's outer skin might react to poison ivy or an insect bite. The airways get red and hot, and they begin to swell. It is like having a rash covering the inside of the tubes.

This swelling quickly narrows the passageways through which air travels. It becomes harder and harder for air to move into the alveoli and back out again. A person with narrowed airways must inhale and exhale with greater force to move air through the system. This force can result in a whistling noise—a wheeze—as air rushes through too-thin passageways. The person may also breathe more quickly or start to pant. If oxygen levels in the blood fall, the person may start to feel breathless.

While the airways are swelling, another change is taking place. Inflamed areas produce a flood of mucus. This is a defense mechanism—the body is trying to flush irritants out of the system. In an attempt to clear the mucus, the person coughs. But coughing requires air, and the person is not getting enough air through his or her swollen passages. The result is a feeble cough that lacks the force to expel the mucus, leaving the person with fluid-filled lungs.

Most of asthma's symptoms come from airway constriction. However, scientists have learned in recent decades that inflammation is the underlying problem. All people with asthma have inflamed airways to some degree, all the time, even if they feel completely fine. The result, explains an article by Partners Asthma Center, is that "the bronchial tubes in asthma are 'twitchy' or easily sent into spasm or narrowing. What makes the bronchial tubes 'twitchy' or vulnerable to a variety of stimuli in the world around us . . . is thought to be the persistent presence of inflammation."[9]

Asthma Attacks

Most of the time, people with asthma have manageable symptoms. They may feel fine, or they may feel a bit uncomfortable, but they are able to get the air they need without too much trouble. Occasionally, though, something irritates a person's airways so much that inflammation increases rapidly. This situation is correctly called an asthma exacerbation but is commonly known as an asthma attack. In an asthma attack, the air passages swell to the point that almost no air gets through within a very short time. They also become clogged with mucus. As a result, the person has trouble both pulling air into the lungs and pushing it out. "Think about what happens if you turn on a spigot and there's a sharp bend in the hose, what happens? The water can't get out of the hose, and stays bottled up at the point of obstruction,"

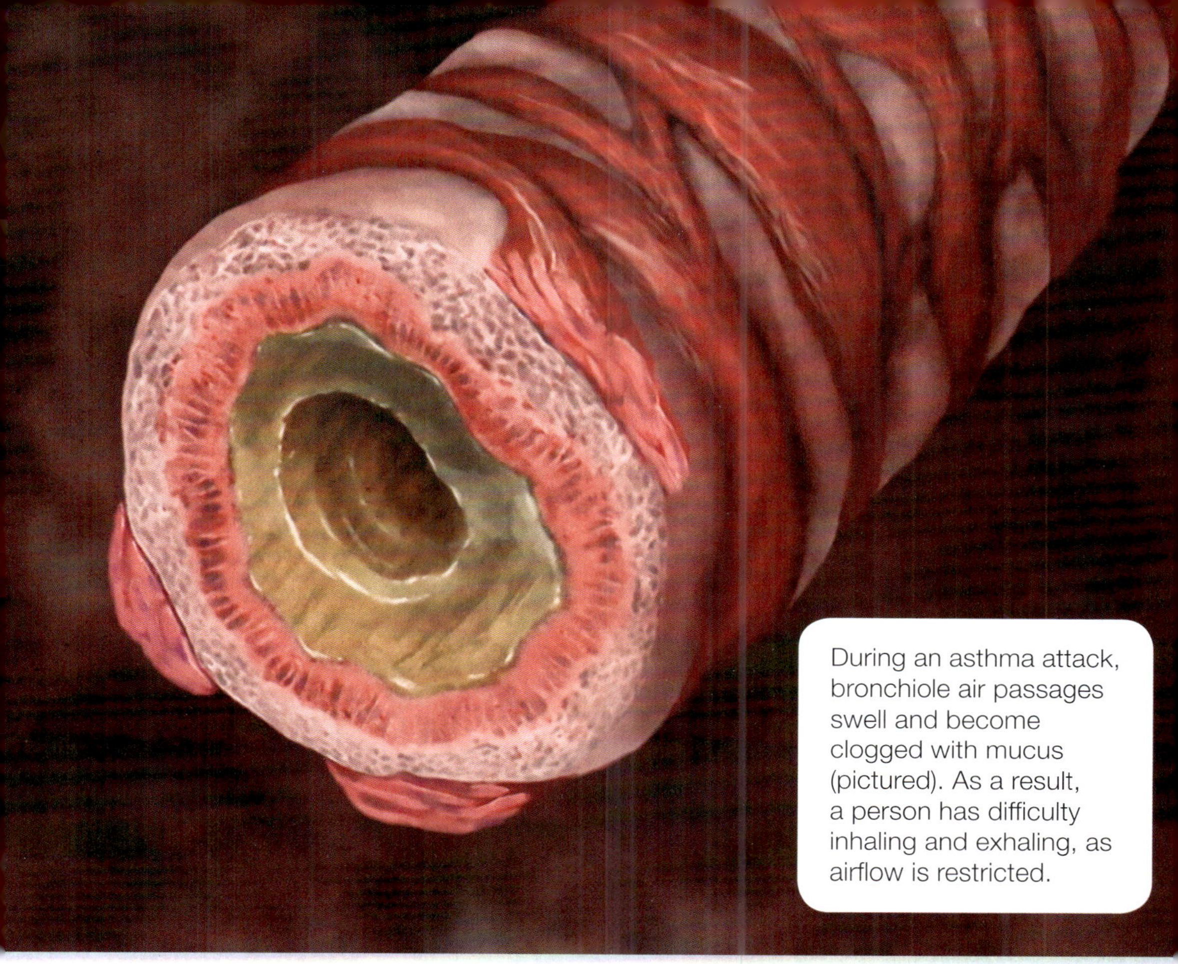

During an asthma attack, bronchiole air passages swell and become clogged with mucus (pictured). As a result, a person has difficulty inhaling and exhaling, as airflow is restricted.

explains Dr. Mehmet Oz of New York-Presbyterian Hospital. "It's the same thing that happens when you have decreased airflow."[10]

Decreased airflow quickly leads to another problem. Carbon dioxide is not being released from the body as it should be, so the levels of this poison build up in the bloodstream. The body responds to this buildup by creating an urgent need to breathe. The person who is experiencing the asthma attack may begin to hyperventilate, which means he or she tries to breathe too rapidly. Because air is not flowing correctly through the person's passageways, however, the rapid attempts to breathe do not have the desired effect. Instead of bringing oxygen into the body, repeated contraction of the chest muscles only irritates the air passages even more. The swelling increases, more mucus is released, and the person's ability to breathe lessens even further.

If the attack continues to intensify, oxygen deprivation may set in. The person's lips and fingertips may turn a bluish shade. The person will feel first light-headed, then very dizzy and may experience vision problems, like spots swimming in front of his or her eyes. By the time these symptoms set in, the person is in immediate danger of losing consciousness. In extreme cases, people can even die from asthma attacks.

This result, fortunately, is not the norm. Most asthma attacks can be brought under control by staying calm and taking fast-acting medications. Still, the experience is frightening. "Very few things are as terrifying as a full blown attack," says Michelle Andrews, who has had severe asthma since she was three years old. "The anxiety that sets in when you can't breathe properly is something non-sufferers will never understand."[11]

Classifying Asthma

Some asthma sufferers, like Andrews, have frequent and severe attacks. Others have only occasional and mild issues. Still others fall somewhere in between these extremes. To describe these differences, an effort called the National Asthma Education and Prevention Program was launched in 1989. The program classifies asthma cases into four categories based on symptoms and severity.

The lowest level of this disorder is called mild intermittent asthma. A person with this type of asthma experiences daytime symptoms two or fewer days a week and nighttime symptoms two or fewer times a month. If the person has asthma attacks at all, they are usually brief. Between attacks, the person has normal airflow into and out of the lungs and no obvious symptoms.

The next level of disease is called mild persistent asthma. Someone in this category experiences symptoms more often than two days a week but no more than once in any individual day and no more than twice a month during the night. Lung function must be at least 80 percent of the disease-free norm. Asthma attacks of any severity may occur and are likely to significantly limit the person's activity when they do.

A History of Asthma

People have been suffering from asthma since the dawn of written history. Prescriptions written in hieroglyphics, for example, have survived from ancient Egypt. These writings mention about seven hundred asthma remedies, one of which is to heat a mixture of herbs on hot bricks and inhale their fumes. In long-ago China, too, certain herbs were inhaled to ease breathing problems.

Asthma was also known to the ancient Greeks. The word *asthma* actually comes from the Greek word *aazein*, which means "to pant," "to exhale with an open mouth," or "to breathe sharply." This condition was first described medically by the Greek physician Hippocrates around 400 BCE in a text called the *Corpus Hippocraticum*. In this text, Hippocrates noted that asthma symptoms were most likely to occur among anglers, tailors, and metalworkers—the first mention of what is now known as occupational asthma.

Another famous physician, Moses Maimonides, explored the condition of asthma around 1200 CE. In a text called *Treatise of Asthma* that described a patient, Prince Al-Afdal, Maimonides noted that his patient's symptoms often started as a common cold during wet months. Eventually, the patient gasped for air and coughed until phlegm was expelled. Maimonides also wrote that the dry months of Egypt helped asthma sufferers.

These writings and others help illustrate the long history of asthma. From ancient days to the present, people have been struggling to manage and overcome this disorder.

One more step up the scale is moderate persistent asthma. In this category, symptoms occur daily, and nighttime symptoms increase, occurring one night or more per week. Measurements of lung function are between 60 percent and 80 percent of the disease-free norm. Increased disease activity or attacks occur at least two times per week, and each episode can last for several days.

The most extreme form of asthma is called severe persistent asthma. In this type of disease, symptoms occur continually, and nighttime symptoms are frequent. Lung function falls to 60 percent or less of the norm. Asthma attacks are frequent and significantly affect a person's daily activities and abilities. Physical exertion often causes attacks, so the person must be very careful about what he or she does.

Asthma Variants

As well as being classified by severity, asthma has several recognized subtypes. Most people have generalized asthma, not a subtype. Subtypes are diagnosed only when a person's disease fits certain narrow criteria.

Cough-variant asthma is a subtype that has cough as the main, and sometimes only, symptom. A person with this disorder has a nagging dry cough that will not go away. It may get worse in chilly weather or if the person catches a cold. The cough can increase at nighttime when the person is lying down. Despite this bothersome cough, however, the person does not wheeze, become breathless, or have asthma attacks, and his or her lung function is normal.

Exercise-induced asthma is another common variant. A person with this condition may develop a dry cough, wheezing, and shortness of breath, along with chest discomfort, during any type of aerobic exercise. The symptoms usually set in when the exercise begins. They often lessen or even disappear during the

A person with exercise-induced asthma may experience wheezing and shortness of breath during aerobic activity like mountain biking. The symptoms set in as the activity begins but often subside as the exercising continues.

course of exercise, but they may recur after the exercise session ends. When the person is not exercising, no symptoms occur.

Aspirin-induced asthma is yet another variant. A person with this condition may experience a severe asthma attack within three hours of taking aspirin or aspirin-like drugs, such as ibuprofen and naproxen. Along with the typical wheezing, cough, and breathlessness, symptoms of an aspirin-induced attack may include a runny nose, puffy eyes, and flushed skin of the face or neck. This type of attack is a medical emergency that may require an emergency room visit or even hospital admission. If left untreated, it can kill.

Occupational asthma is the final common variant. It results from exposure to a specific substance in a person's daily environment. For children, this can include substances encountered at school or in day care. Outside this environment, the person with this subtype does not experience asthma symptoms—but in the environment, the person feels constantly ill. It may take months or years for problems to kick in. Once they do, however, they tend to persist. "It takes very little exposure once you're sensitized to provoke symptoms," explains allergist John Santilli. "As time goes on, it takes more and more out of you, and you get sicker and sicker."[12]

When Does Asthma Emerge?

Although asthma can emerge at any age, from infancy to adulthood, symptoms most commonly surface in early childhood. Several studies have found that anywhere from 50 percent to 80 percent of children with asthma develop symptoms before their fifth birthday. These symptoms, however, are often mistaken for other conditions, such as recurrent colds, sinus infections, or allergies. The child may not be diagnosed with asthma until obvious attacks start to occur. If the child's condition stays mild and no attacks occur, asthma can go undetected and undiagnosed for decades.

Asthma that is diagnosed after age twenty is called adult-onset asthma. Many people who receive this diagnosis probably did have asthma as children, but the condition was mild enough to go unrecognized. "I see people in my office all the time who say they never had breathing problems before—until I ask about their symptoms during childhood. Many remember holding on to colds longer than their friends, experiencing trouble running in cold weather, or having colds settling in their chests. These people probably had very mild, intermittent asthma,"[13] says Dr. Anna Feldweg of Brigham and Women's Hospital in Boston.

> **"I see people in my office all the time who say they never had breathing problems before—until I ask about their symptoms during childhood."[13]**
>
> —Anna Feldweg, a physician at Brigham and Women's Hospital

In many adult-onset cases, a change in the person's environment or health has increased airway inflammation, which in turn leads to asthma. Common triggers include hormonal changes such as those that occur during pregnancy, allergies, environmental irritants like smoke and dust, and certain illnesses, particularly a bad cold or the flu. Any of these things can kick-start the breathlessness, wheezing, and coughing associated with asthma.

Infants and Asthma

Older children, teens, and adults with asthma can describe their symptoms to doctors. Babies and preverbal toddlers, on the other hand, cannot tell anyone when something is wrong. They also cannot describe their precise feelings and symptoms. For this reason, asthma that emerges during the earliest years of a child's life can be tricky to detect and diagnose. A baby who coughs, wheezes, or seems short of breath may have asthma, but it also could be a number of other conditions.

To diagnose asthma in very young children, doctors therefore look for additional signs. Some red flags include lethargic activity and poor responses to one's surroundings, such as not recognizing or responding to parents; difficulty nursing or eating; soft, shallow crying; and flaring nostrils. When a baby is experiencing more severe symptoms, his or her chest may heave as the muscles contract over and over, trying to draw air. In emergency situations, the baby may develop a blue tinge to the skin due to oxygen deprivation. Called cyanosis, this development is a medical emergency that requires immediate treatment.

After these symptoms and others lead to a diagnosis, infant asthma becomes a bit easier to monitor. Most parents learn to recognize the symptoms quickly and take action to ease them. Because asthma symptoms can occur without much outward sign, however, some parents use stethoscopes to listen to their babies' lungs. With the right tools and proper training, anyone can hear the telltale wheezing of asthma long before obvious symptoms appear.

Asthma Outlook

It is vitally important to stay on top of infant or youth asthma in this way and others. Uncontrolled asthma causes repeated flare-ups of inflammation in the airways. These episodes can damage the airways and lead to scarring, which is called airway fibrosis. Airway fibrosis develops very slowly, over a long period. Once it occurs, however, the damage cannot be undone. It causes a permanent narrowing of the airways, called remodeling, that will affect a person's breathing forever.

The shorter-term effects of asthma, too, are important to monitor. Severe asthma attacks are life-threatening emergencies that can and do kill people—about ten per day in the United States alone. Medical professionals point out, however, that most people who die from asthma develop progressive symptoms—meaning they get worse and worse—at least twelve hours and up to several weeks before the fatal attack. In other words, says physician Pat Bass of the Louisiana State University Health Sciences Center, "The vast majority of patients dying from asthma developed symptoms in a time frame that would have allowed them to seek appropriate medical care."[14]

Receiving appropriate care, unfortunately, can be difficult for some children with asthma. Not everyone has health insurance or access to good doctors. In the United States poverty is strongly linked to uncontrolled childhood asthma and to asthma deaths. In low-income and undeveloped nations around the world, the situation is similar. Parents who cannot afford doctor visits may be forced to manage their children's asthma symptoms on their own. This is a huge risk that in some cases can have deadly results.

> **"The vast majority of patients dying from asthma developed symptoms in a time frame that would have allowed them to seek appropriate medical care."[14]**
>
> —Pat Bass, a physician at Louisiana State University Health Sciences Center

The good news is that as the global incidence of asthma has increased, awareness is rising, and efforts are being made to educate the public about this health threat. In the United States, for example, the CDC's National Asthma Control Program funds states, school programs, and various asthma-related organizations to help them improve surveillance of asthma, train health professionals, educate individuals with asthma and their families, and explain asthma to the public. There is every hope that this initiative, and others like it around the world, will help children with asthma breathe easier.

Chapter 2

What Causes Asthma?

When it comes to asthma, it seems everyone has a different opinion about the causes of their particular case. On an Internet message board, people compare notes and try to pin down these causes. "My youngest sister was diagnosed with asthma when she was 8 or 9 years old. I wasn't diagnosed until my early 20s. My father was diagnosed even later, in his early 50s I believe. However, I think he had it in his youth because of the stories he told me of his near death experiences he had when he was a child,"[15] says one poster, who is convinced that the disorder runs in his family.

A different poster blames her asthma on environmental influences. "I grew up in a home where smoking and pets were in abundance. . . . [The incidence of asthma] does seem to be increasing with all of the environmental toxins as well as the climate and the changes that seem to be happening on that front," she says. "I also have allergies to all kinds of trees and grass and that has been very extreme for the past few years for me."[16]

Yet another poster believes her asthma is the result of her diet during infancy. "I am the first case of asthma in my family. . . . I don't know what caused it in particular, but I suspect strongly from the [formula] I drank as a baby because my mum [chose] not to breastfeed me,"[17] she says.

These people have very different theories about the causes of their asthma—and they may all be right. Scientists have done a great deal of research on this topic, and they now understand that many factors, both genetic and environmental, can contribute to the development of asthma.

Running in the Family

The first question researchers ask about any disorder is whether children can inherit it from their parents. In the case of asthma, the answer is a clear yes. "If one of your biologic parents has or had asthma, then you are more likely to develop asthma than if he or she did not have asthma. If both of your parents have asthma, you are even more likely to develop asthma than if only one parent has this condition,"[18] explains the website of Partners Asthma Center in Boston, Massachusetts.

Studies of a disorder's heritability—the tendency to be passed from parent to child—focus on the makeup of deoxyribonucleic acid (DNA), a protein that acts as the body's instruction book. It contains all the information a person needs to develop, live, and reproduce. DNA can be further broken down into genes, which are small regions of the DNA that affect specific traits. For instance, a gene might control a person's eye color, height, blood type, or other physical characteristics—such as the tendency to develop asthma.

> **"If one of your biologic parents has or had asthma, then you are more likely to develop asthma."[18]**
>
> —Partners Asthma Center, Boston, Massachusetts

One way to study genes' effects is to compare the health of identical and fraternal twins. Twins studies are based on the fact that identical twins share identical DNA and genetics, while fraternal twins are no more closely related than non-twin siblings.

Twins studies are often used to help determine the genetic inheritability of disorders. These and other genetic studies strongly support a hereditary link to asthma.

Both types of twins, however, did share the same environment and influences in the womb. When the twins are raised together, they also have very similar postbirth environment and experiences. If significant differences exist in certain disorders between identical and fraternal twins, therefore, genetics are likely to be the primary reason.

It turns out that such differences do exist in asthma. If one identical twin has asthma, the other twin has a 25 percent chance of having asthma as well—about three times greater than children in the general population. Fraternal twins, on the other hand, are no more likely than non-twin siblings to have asthma.

Although twins studies and other genetic studies strongly support a hereditary link to asthma, there does not seem to be one single gene linked to this disorder. At last count, scientists had discovered at least one hundred genes that seem to play a role in

The Hygiene Hypothesis

Germ-phobic parents work hard to keep their homes as clean as possible for their babies and children—but according to a theory called the hygiene hypothesis, a too-clean environment may actually increase a child's risk of asthma. LiveScience writer Alina Bradford explains how it works.

> The idea is simple. When babies are inside the womb they have a very weak immune system because they are given protection by their mother's antibodies. When they exit the womb, though, the immune system must start working for itself. For the immune system to work properly, it is thought that the child must be exposed to germs so that it has a chance to strengthen. . . .
>
> The idea is similar to the training of a body builder. For a body builder to be able to lift heavy objects, the muscles must be trained by lifting heavier and heavier objects. If the body builder never trains, then he will be unable to lift a heavy object when asked. The same is thought to be true for the immune system. [To be] able to fight off infection, the immune system must train by fighting off contaminants found in everyday life.

The hygiene hypothesis was proposed by scientist David P. Strachan in the late 1980s. It has come under fire in recent years from scientists who claim that although Strachan makes an important point, the hygiene hypothesis paints too simple a picture. Too-clean conditions may contribute to asthma—but they are just one factor among many.

Alina Bradford, "What Is the Hygiene Hypothesis?," LiveScience, March 17, 2016. www.livescience.com.

asthma—and that number continues to grow as new discoveries are made. These genes interact in complex ways to determine the symptoms and severity of each individual's asthma.

In the Womb

Genetics may play a strong role in the development of asthma, but a person's DNA is far from the only factor. Environmental influences also play an important role—and research shows that some of these influences occur in the womb, before the fetus even enters the world.

Chemicals called phthalates exert one such influence. Phthalates are used to soften plastics. They are found in vinyl flooring, food containers, and many other commonly encountered items. A recent study monitored phthalate levels in the bodies of three hundred pregnant women, then tracked the women's babies after they were born. The study found that the children of high-phthalate mothers had up to a 78 percent greater chance of developing asthma than children with low-phthalate mothers.

Acetaminophen, the active ingredient in Tylenol, is another chemical that may have a negative effect on unborn babies. Studies have found a correlation between a pregnant mother's use of this drug and the incidence of asthma in her children after they are born. Scientists caution that no link has been proved, and they point out that correlation is not the same thing as causation. Still, says physician Ari Brown, "Considering that several studies have found similar results, it makes sense for . . . pregnant women to take acetaminophen only when they absolutely need it."[19]

A pregnant mother's stress level is yet another factor that may influence her unborn child. A 2010 study questioned 557 pregnant women about the amounts and types of stress in their lives. When these women's babies were born, researchers tested their blood to see how it responded to allergens. They discovered that the babies of high-stress mothers produced high levels of an inflammation-causing chemical, while the babies of low-stress mothers produced low levels of the same chemical. This finding, the study concluded, was an indicator of how well the babies' immune systems were working at birth, which in turn was a predictive factor for the babies' chances of developing asthma.

Allergy Development

Once a baby is born, other factors come into play. Environmental influences are particularly important during a child's earliest years because the lungs of a newborn, especially the alveoli, are not fully developed. In fact, the large majority of a person's alveoli—about 85 percent—form between birth and age three. Mucus-producing cells and blood vessels that support the alveoli also develop during this period. Anything that harms this process can have permanent effects on the child's respiratory system, which in turn can increase the child's risk of asthma.

The biggest risk during this critical period is exposure to allergens. Allergens are substances that tend to cause allergic responses. Allergies develop when these substances enter a person's bloodstream. There they encounter antibodies, which are proteins that patrol the blood, looking for dangerous intruders such as viruses and bacteria. If the antibodies decide a certain allergen is a threat, they may attack it. This kicks off a process that results in the person's immune system becoming sensitive to that allergen. From that point onward, if the allergen enters the person's body, an immune response will occur. Allergic immune responses can result in many symptoms, including breathlessness, wheezing, coughing, and airway narrowing—in other words, asthma symptoms. These symptoms, in turn, can damage lung development and increase the child's risk of severe asthma going forward.

Atopy

Although anyone can have allergies, children with a condition called atopy are at much greater risk. Atopy is a genetic tendency to develop allergies. It is most often passed down from mothers to their children, although fathers can also contribute genes for atopy. Children with atopy are not born with allergies; they must have contact with an allergen before a hypersensitivity reaction can occur. Once this type of contact occurs, however, these children are much more likely to have severe reactions.

Atopy usually presents in three ways. People with this condition may have eczema (also called atopic dermatitis), allergic rhinitis (hay fever), or allergic asthma. Some unfortunate people have all three conditions, in what is called the allergic triad. "I . . . have all three (four if you count food allergies)," says Kenzie, a young woman who fits this description. "I am allergic to everything flowery, whether it be nature or perfume. I am also allergic to a few foods and my skin is very very sensitive. And to top it all off I have asthma, which affects me daily."[20] For Kenzie and many others, atopy is the genetic springboard that leads to asthma misery.

Allergens in the Home

Certain foods are particularly likely to cause allergies. About 90 percent of all food allergies come from eight foods: cow's milk, eggs, peanuts, tree nuts, fish, shellfish, soy, and wheat. If babies or young toddlers consume these foods while their systems are vulnerable and still developing, allergies can easily arise. These allergies increase the child's risk of future asthma.

Besides food, many other asthma triggers are found in the home environment. Among the worst and most common triggers are dust mites. These microscopic, spiderlike creatures feed on the skin flakes of human beings. They tend to swarm anywhere people are shedding their skin, such as in the fabric of couches, beds, stuffed animals, and clothing. Scientists say that the typical bed is crawling with 1 million to 2 million dust mites, and pillows are even worse—about 10 percent of the weight of a well-used pillow comes from dead skin cells, mites, and mite droppings. An estimated 75 percent of people with allergic asthma are sensitive to proteins made by these creatures.

Household pets also produce proteins that can trigger asthma. These proteins are found in shed skin particles, which is called dander. They are also found in urine and saliva. All types of furry and feathered pets—including dogs, cats, rodents, rabbits, ferrets, and even horses and birds—produce these proteins and can cause asthma in people who are susceptible to them. "I'm highly allergic to cats and have had a couple of cat induced asthma attacks where I could not breathe and needed an inhaler. That was mostly in environments that had not been recently cleaned/vacuumed,"[21] explains an asthma sufferer named Kate. The lack of recent cleaning meant pet dander was abundant and caused this young woman's asthma symptoms.

> **"I'm highly allergic to cats and have had a couple of cat induced asthma attacks where I could not breathe and needed an inhaler."[21]**
>
> —Kate, asthma sufferer

Mold is yet another asthma trigger often found inside people's homes. Mold grows from microscopic spores that drift in from outdoors or are carried inside on people's bodies and clothing. If the spores settle in damp places, such as bathrooms, kitchens, and basements, they may begin to grow. An established mold colony releases more spores, which float through the air and into people's airways—where they can cause allergy attacks and asthma symptoms.

Cigarette Smoke

The impacts of food, dust mites, pets, and mold pale in comparison to the number one indoor asthma trigger: cigarette smoke. Most children do not smoke, but the people they live with may. The smoke that is released directly from a burning cigarette, as well as the smoke breathed out by people, is called secondhand smoke. Secondhand tobacco smoke contains about seven thousand chemicals, many of which can irritate the lungs and airways of those who are nearby. "People were smoking near me. My chest got really tight. I was trying to breathe, trying to get air into my lungs. I couldn't bear it,"[22] recalls an asthmatic teen named Jamason, whose condition is strongly triggered by cigarette smoke.

> **"People were smoking near me. My chest got really tight. I was trying to breathe, trying to get air into my lungs."[22]**
>
> —Jamason, asthma sufferer

There is yet another type of smoking residue called thirdhand smoke. Thirdhand smoke consists of tiny chemical particles that settle onto surfaces in the home and linger for months. Unlike secondhand smoke, thirdhand smoke cannot be eliminated by blowing fans or opening windows and doors. It sticks to everything. It breaks free bit by bit over time, escaping into the air and then into human noses.

Statistics show a clear link between secondhand and thirdhand smoke and childhood asthma. Wheezing and coughing are much more common in children who are exposed regularly to cigarette smoke. Secondhand smoke can also trigger asthma attacks; children who live with smokers have more asthma attacks than those who do not, and in fact, more than 40 percent of children who end up in the emergency room with asthma live with smokers. As time

Cigarette smoke is known to be the number one indoor asthma trigger. Statistics show a clear link between secondhand smoke and childhood asthma.

goes on and smoke exposure continues, studies show, children who live with smokers get sick more often and are more prone to lung diseases like bronchitis and pneumonia. Their lungs also grow less than those of children not exposed to secondhand smoke. These effects, in turn, increase these children's incidence of asthma.

Sick Schools

The phrase "sick building syndrome," or SBS for short, describes a situation in which people in a building become ill or feel unwell for no apparent reason. When they leave the building, the symptoms disappear. Scientists estimate that about one-third of US schools suffer from SBS, with air quality problems severe enough to cause asthma in students and teachers.

There are five main warning signs that a school building may be sick, as listed below:

mold: Seeing or smelling mold is a red flag that must be addressed immediately. Visible mold usually signals a much larger growth within walls or in other dark, damp, nonvisible areas.

dust: Dust under lockers, in room corners, on top of bulletin boards, and in other nooks and crannies is a sign of dusty air and generally poor air quality.

idling buses: If buses idle for a long time, their exhaust can drift into doors and windows or through air intakes. These harmful fumes can trigger asthma symptoms.

blocked heating and cooling units: Heating and cooling units not only control the temperature, they also create airflow. Good airflow is important for air quality.

toxic cleaning products: The fumes from some cleaning products can make indoor air even more polluted than outdoor city air. Schools should always use "green" cleaning products that are certified fume-free.

School officials often complain that they do not have enough money to solve problems like these. It is true that schools are underfunded. But if they cannot maintain their buildings, poor air quality is sure to result—and the students, teachers, and staff will feel it with every burning, wheezing breath.

Outdoor Allergens

Outside the home, more allergens lurk. One of the most common outdoor allergens is pollen, which is a fine powder released from some trees, grasses, and weeds. The amount of pollen in the air varies from time to time, being highest during the spring and summer and lowest during nongrowth times of the year, particularly wintertime in cold regions. According to one estimate, about 80 percent of people with asthma report that pollen triggers their symptoms.

Air pollution, too, is a very common outdoor trigger. Air pollution can take many forms. One problem in asthma is ozone, a gas that contributes to smog or haze. It is most common in cities with heavy automobile traffic and tends to build up on hot, still summer days. Ozone is very irritating to the lungs and airways and is directly linked to asthma attacks and emergency room visits. This gas can also reduce lung function, making it even harder for people with asthma to breathe freely.

Airborne particles can also cause asthma. Airborne particles may come from human-made sources, such as smokestacks and vehicle exhaust. They may also come from natural sources, such as volcanic eruptions, forest fires, and dust storms. Whatever their source, airborne particles can be breathed into the lungs, where they cause irritation that can lead to asthma. Long-term exposure does the most damage, but even short-term exposure can cause asthma symptoms and attacks.

Outdoor mold is yet another allergen. Like mold in the home, outdoor mold releases microscopic spores into the air. If conditions are right, the spores can drift for long distances. They may eventually find their way into a person's lungs, where they can cause the symptoms of asthma.

Viral Infections

For many people, allergens are a constant irritant that lead to nearly continuous low-level asthma symptoms. To bring on a really serious attack, though, something more may be needed. That extra push often comes in the form of viral respiratory infections, such as the common cold or influenza. According to some estimates, these illnesses cause a whopping 85 percent of childhood asthma attacks and 50 percent of adult attacks. They also may be responsible for up to 70 percent of all asthma-related hospital admissions.

Respiratory infections themselves do not cause asthma symptoms. The problem is the body's immune response as it tries to fight the illness. When invading viruses are detected, the body releases chemicals that inflame the upper airways and make them swell. It also stimulates certain cells to produce mucus. The swelling traps viruses, and the mucus surrounds them, making gooey balls that can be swallowed and then destroyed in the stomach's acid bath.

This process is vital for the body's good health, but it is not pleasant. Even nonasthmatic people feel miserable when their airways are hot, swollen, raw, and clogged with mucus. For a person with asthma, however, this situation can be devastating. The person's already hypersensitive airways may have an extreme reaction to the immune onslaught. They become grossly overswollen and "twitchy," a word doctors use to describe hypersensitive reactions in the airways. Without prompt medical care, the situation can develop into a severe asthma attack that can put the person in grave danger.

To prevent this from happening, people with asthma must do their best to avoid getting sick. They should stay away from those who are ill and get annual flu shots. If they do catch a cold or the flu, they should contact their doctor, particularly if asthma symptoms develop. Mild symptoms can quickly worsen, so it is important to make sure they are well controlled.

Even More Triggers

Even if a person somehow manages to avoid all allergens and illnesses, other unavoidable triggers exist. The weather is one

Although cold air is the most common weather-related asthma trigger, other weather conditions can cause problems as well. Abrupt temperature changes, high humidity, wind, and thunderstorms can all induce asthma symptoms for some people.

such trigger. Cold, dry air is particularly likely to cause asthma symptoms, since it both dehydrates the airways and stimulates mucus production. Dehydrated airways are more likely to become irritated, and increased mucus flow clogs the already susceptible system. "As an asthma and allergy sufferer I dread winter the most! I can't even walk outside without fearing my lungs will begin to close up,"[23] says one person whose condition flares up in cold weather.

> **"I dread winter the most! I can't even walk outside without fearing my lungs will begin to close up."[23]**
>
> —Asthma sufferer

Although cold air is the most common asthma trigger, other weather conditions can cause problems as well. Abrupt temperature changes, fog, high humidity, wind, and thunderstorms can all cause asthma symptoms or attacks in some people. In short, anything that affects the air going into people's lungs can affect asthma as well.

While weather changes the environment outside the body, chemicals called hormones work from within. Hormones are messengers that control most major bodily functions. Their levels fluctuate constantly to adjust to the body's needs—and these fluctuations can be linked to asthma symptoms. In particular, asthmatic female teens and women may be more likely to develop symptoms during certain parts of their menstrual cycle. Pregnancy and menopause, which both change the body's hormonal balance, can also affect a person's asthma—usually for the worse, but sometimes for the better. "My doctor said that one-third of women see a decrease of asthma symptoms, one-third have symptoms that stay the same . . . and one-third have asthma symptoms that get worse. So far, I seem to be in the third whose symptoms actually improve while pregnant,"[24] one woman says on popular pregnancy website the Bump.

Strong emotions can be yet another hard-to-control asthma trigger. Negative emotions such as anger, sadness, worry, and stress cause the body to release a hormone called cortisol. Cortisol suppresses the immune system, which can contribute to an increase in asthma symptoms. Negative emotions also increase a person's heart rate and blood pressure, which can contribute to airway inflammation and narrowing.

Even positive emotions can trigger asthma. Some people find that their airways constrict after vigorous laughing or exciting experiences. For these people, staying calm is an important asthma management strategy.

Ongoing Research

In addition to the main asthma triggers, there are many others as well. Asthma can be aggravated by a variety of other things, including exercise, cleaning products, medicines, strong scents, workplace fumes and building materials, and much more. It is fair to say that anything that affects the airways, either by a person's actions or simply by getting breathed in, can lead to asthma symptoms. The triggers are different for each person and can vary from one time of life to another.

Because this disorder is so highly variable, scientists have had a hard time pinning down asthma's exact causes. Ongoing research, however, is trying to shed some light on this question. Some current studies, for example, are examining specific gene variations to see if they might predict how a patient will respond to different asthma medications and which patients are more susceptible to having severe attacks. Other studies are trying to determine how certain immune cells cause allergic sensitization. Still other studies are looking at the role of viral infections and environmental influences on asthma symptoms.

Asthma is so complex that it may never be completely understood—but each advance in knowledge is one more piece of the puzzle. With continued study and attention, this disorder will be better and better understood. This in turn will allow the medical community to help asthmatic patients live healthy, happy, and relatively symptom-free lives.

Chapter 3

What Is It like to Live with Asthma?

John Bottrell is a respiratory therapist who feels deep empathy for his patients—because he has severe asthma himself. In an online article, Bottrell shared his thoughts on living with asthma.

> Can you really live a normal life with asthma? Maybe most asthmatics can live a normal life. Yet there remain a bunch of asthmatics like me who have to make adjustments. . . . Think of it this way. A normal person can make a split decision to leave the house and not have to think "Do I have my inhaler with me? Did I take all my medicine?" A normal guy can go to the cabin on a whim and stay for a week without thinking anything about it other than having fun. . . . A normal guy can run if he wants. A normal guy can eat the foods he wants without having to worry about allergies. A normal guy can saw wood or rip up old carpet if he wants. A normal guy can cut the grass and pull weeds. A normal guy can rake the yard without having to stop to use his inhaler.[25]

Despite these limitations, Bottrell maintains that living with asthma is not so bad. "Life is what you make of it. . . . Yes, you'll probably have to make some adjustments, but you can still live a relatively normal life with asthma."[26]

Around the world, asthmatic people of all ages struggle with this challenge every day. Each person must find a way to manage his or her symptoms. While asthma is a little different for everyone, there are some common challenges faced by many people who suffer from this disorder.

Struggling to Breathe

Breathing difficulties are the hallmark of asthma. Nearly everyone with an asthma diagnosis has this problem at least occasionally, while others have it constantly.

A teen named Nicole is among the lucky ones. She has very mild asthma that affects her only once or twice a year on average. She was diagnosed at age five when a viral infection sent her to late-night urgent care with a high fever, wheezing, and breathlessness. "I remember the doctor gave me a treatment to help my breathing. She told my mom that I had asthma, and she prescribed medicine that I could take anytime I felt short of breath," she recalls. "That was ten years ago. I still use the medicine every now and then, but I hardly ever need it. My asthma really doesn't bother me much."[27]

> **"The shortness of breath and the coughing are the things that trouble me most."[28]**
>
> —Peter, asthma sufferer

A man named Peter, who has been coping with asthma since childhood, has more constant symptoms. "The shortness of breath and the coughing are the things that trouble me most. It may be mild and I might not notice it until I'm sort of walking up a steep hill for a few minutes or it may affect me just going up a few stairs. And I may not be able to hold a normal conversation because I haven't got enough breath to keep it going,"[28] he says. Although Peter has never had a serious asthma flare-up, his symptoms still have a significant impact on his daily life.

Millions of other people around the world are in a similar situation. They use different words to describe the feeling of constant breathlessness. They may say they feel like a fish out of water, like an elephant is sitting on their chest, or like a pillow is being held over their face. A young woman named Theresa Cannizzaro colorfully says her asthma feels "like I am wearing a really tight corset while trying to breathe through a coffee stirrer straw."[29] For those with frequent symptoms, living with asthma is one long struggle to breathe.

When Asthma Attacks

While all people with asthma experience symptoms, not everyone has asthma attacks. The CDC reports that in 2015, the most recent year for which numbers are available, 46.9 percent of Americans with asthma had an attack. Children tended to have slightly higher rates of attacks (47.5 percent) than adults (46.6 percent).

By all accounts, an asthma attack is a terrifying experience. A young woman named Michelle Andrews, who has been suffering from severe asthma since age three, describes in vivid detail what an asthma attack is like for her:

> I can't breathe and my medication isn't working *and I can't breathe*. . . . I close my eyes and do everything I can to inhale through my nose while [my boyfriend] races around, grabbing everything we'll need for the hospital. My mind is racing. I put my head between my legs . . . all I can think about is my lungs. If I could speak, I'd calmly say my lungs aren't working. They're just not working. I need air. Can you please do something to get me air? I'm starting to feel dizzy. There are black dots everywhere.
>
> Now I panic. *Really panic*. I need my lungs to work again so I breathe as fast and as deep as I can. Faster and faster

> and faster. Pins and needles spread across my body and my legs and arms become stiff. I hear my own breathing . . . I'm hyperventilating and I can't stop. I need air. I really need air. I can't breathe.[30]

Staying calm is usually the key to bringing an asthma attack under control. If a person relaxes and breathes very slowly and gently, the inflammation normally subsides enough for air to pass. Fast-acting medications can help the process. But it is not easy for anyone, particularly children, to stay calm and relaxed when they feel like they are suffocating. It usually takes years of experience before a person understands his or her body well enough to manage an asthma attack without panicking. And, of course, not all asthma attacks can be managed. The worst attacks can kill, and this fact adds an edge of fear even for people with years of asthma experience.

Staying calm and practicing slow, gentle breathing is usually the key to bringing an asthma attack under control. Fast-acting medications, like those delivered through an inhaler, can also help reduce the inflammation in the airways.

Writer Vann R. Newkirk II, who has asthma, neatly sums up this reality. "Having severe or poorly controlled frequent asthma is a ceaseless cycle of fear," he explains. "Quite simply, asthma can be a nightmare, even between attacks."[31]

Sick All the Time

Fear, of course, is far from the only issue. Asthma's symptoms take a heavy physical toll. Between asthma attacks and milder symptoms, children with asthma can feel poorly most or all of the time. They may not sleep well at night due to coughing, which

Overcoming Asthma

Many famous people have asthma but have learned to control their symptoms and overcome this disorder. This short sampling of asthmatic celebrities demonstrates that it is possible to survive and thrive despite having asthma.

Jessica Alba, actor
David Beckham, professional soccer player
Bono, lead vocalist of U2
Alice Cooper, rock singer
DMX, rapper
Eminem, rapper, songwriter
Jackie Joyner-Kersee, Olympic medalist in track
Pink, singer
Dennis Rodman, professional basketball player
Harry Styles, singer and actor
Isaiah Thomas, professional basketball player
Kristi Yamaguchi, Olympic medalist in figure skating

Among US presidents, asthma is more common than it is in the general population. Bill Clinton, Calvin Coolidge, John F. Kennedy, Theodore Roosevelt, Martin Van Buren, and Woodrow Wilson—representing 13.33 percent of the US presidential pool—all have or had asthma.

makes them exhausted and lethargic during the day. They may have very low energy levels due to both tiredness and insufficient oxygen in their bloodstream. They may also have trouble concentrating, either because they are tired or because the medications they take for their asthma symptoms make their head spin or cause other physical side effects. It is very difficult for a child in this circumstance to do well in school, participate in extracurricular activities, or have a normal social life.

For children with severe asthma, medical care can be an overwhelming part of life. Statistics from the CDC illustrate the scope of this problem. According to the most recent available data, which is not broken down by age, asthma in the United States alone accounts for about 10.5 million doctor visits, 1.6 million emergency room visits, and 1.3 million hospital outpatient visits per year. There were nearly 137,000 asthma-related hospital admissions of children under age eighteen. This number covers all admissions, not all patients. Certain children who are very ill may be admitted multiple times over the course of the year, and each admission is counted toward the total.

Not surprisingly, the symptoms and management of asthma cause children with this disorder to miss a great deal of school. Childhood asthma is the leading cause of school absenteeism in the United States, with up to 14 million missed school days each year. This can make it hard for children with asthma to keep up academically and get good grades.

Constant illness also affects the parents who must care for severely asthmatic children. A mother named Esther describes the toll her child's asthma has taken on her own life. "When she was eighteen months old she became asthmatic. She had some episodes where we were in hospital, and from then on my life wasn't really my own. . . . [I] couldn't go back to work because I knew that I wouldn't be able to keep a job down, because at any minute the nightmare might begin where she would be poorly and I'd spend three days just looking after her,"[32] she explains. For this child's family and many others, living with asthma has a ripple effect that impacts everyone involved.

Physical Activity

Most children and teens with asthma are not constantly ill. Their symptoms come and go, or are aggravated only by certain triggers. Vigorous physical activity is one such trigger. Young people with asthma may find that they become breathless or wheeze during physical education classes at school or when playing with friends after school hours. They may tend to shy away from exercise as a result.

Asthma and Olympic Athletic Performance

Can people with asthma really become top athletes? The answer is a resounding yes. Statistics show, in fact, that asthmatic athletes outperform those without asthma in the Olympics, winning a disproportionate amount of medals—particularly in winter sports. It may be that the extra effort and discipline needed to train with asthma translates into higher performance when it really counts.

Percentage of Athletes with Asthma and Corresponding Percentage of Individual Medals Won by Athletes with Asthma at the Olympic Games, 2000–2010

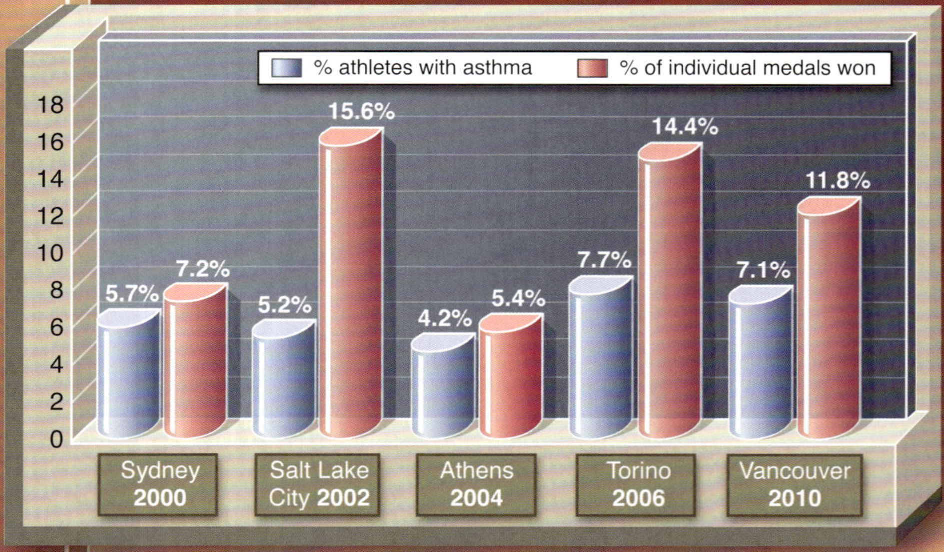

Source: Ken Fitch, "The World Anti-Doping Code: Can You Have Asthma and Still Be an Elite Athlete?," *Breathe*, June 2016. www.ncbi.nlm.nih.gov.

Medical professionals emphasize that avoiding exercise is not the right answer for children with asthma. Physical exertion helps people become stronger, boosts the immune system, and improves lung function. All of these effects can improve asthma symptoms in the long run. Still, young people with asthma need to be sensible with exercise and know their limitations. They may choose activities such as yoga or walking, which do not cause as much panting as running or other highly aerobic sports.

"I do not let sports take over my life, and if I can't breathe easily, I will take a break from the sport or go back to my doctor and see what is wrong."[34]

—Kat, asthma sufferer

For those who do choose vigorous sports, asthma symptoms must be carefully monitored and controlled. A teen athlete named Kat, who plays soccer and runs cross-country, explains how she manages her asthma:

> Whenever I feel breathing trouble about to start, I take a puff on my inhaler. I do this even in the middle of a soccer game, which I really don't like but know I need to do! Before every sporting event I take two puffs on my inhaler. And because cold air will make my asthma worse, I wear a ski mask over my face when I'm outside or competing. I wear the mask because it warms the air before I breathe it.[33]

Although Kat is dedicated to her teams, she also understands that taking care of herself is her number one priority. "I do not let sports take over my life, and if I can't breathe easily, I will take a break from the sport or go back to my doctor and see what is wrong,"[34] she explains. With constant attention to her asthma, Kat manages to stay active and mostly symptom-free.

I Cannot Do That

Although Kat can work around her asthma to continue the sports she loves, this is not always possible for all kids. Some young people simply cannot do certain types of exercise without bringing on an asthma attack. Other children may be fine with exercise but might not be able to do other things. A person who develops asthma symptoms around horses, for instance, would be wise to refrain from horseback riding or carriage rides. Someone who is triggered by cats or dogs might not be able to have a pet. Limitations like these are something that every person with asthma has to deal with in one way or another.

On Internet message boards, several people talk about the things they cannot do because of their asthma. "I would love to sing in a choir. I used to sing when I was younger and I can't because I don't know from . . . one month to the next whether my breathing's going to behave or not. I don't feel I would be reliable enough,"[35] says Eve, a woman who has suffered from asthma for nearly two decades.

Another poster is strongly triggered by dust and cleaning products. "I can't clean my room . . . or else I go into coughing fits and it gets worse from there. Mind you, this happens even if I [wear] a mask,"[36] he says.

Yet another person talks about discouraging side effects from his asthma medications. "I . . . take long term medications which give me [a high heart rate], so I can't for example drink caffeine. It's those little things that make this seem very hard and seem like it will limit my ability to experience life to the fullest,"[37] he explains.

Limitations like these can be very depressing for anyone living with asthma. It is particularly hard for children and teens, who usually care strongly about fitting in with their peers. It can be hard for them not to feel sad and discouraged when they cannot do things that others take for granted.

Asthma Camps

Healthy children head off to summer camps with very few second thoughts. For asthmatic youth, however, summer camps can be a terrifying minefield of asthma triggers. Rustic and outdoor accommodations can be awash in allergens, including pollen, dust, insect droppings, and mold. Campfires are a source of smoke. Hiking, swimming, and other vigorous activities can aggravate symptoms for those who are sensitive to exercise. Horseback riding and other animal-related activities can be yet another problem area.

Recognizing these issues, summer camps that cater specifically to children with asthma have sprung up in recent decades. There are now about 120 such camps in America, serving more than ten thousand children each year. The activities and environment at these camps are designed to minimize asthma triggers. The counselors are all respiratory therapists and nurses who can keep a trained medical eye on the campers. Along with traditional camp activities, asthma camps also devote part of each day to educating campers about how to manage their condition.

Surveys have been done to assess the success of asthma camps. These surveys have found that attendees report better use of asthma management tools, are more likely to be using medicines to keep their symptoms under control, and assume more responsibility for taking their medications in a proper and timely manner. Just as important, the attendees report that they are having fun. By allowing asthmatic kids to have a typical summer camp experience, asthma camps make it just a little easier to live with asthma.

Constant Monitoring

The sheer time and attention required to keep asthma under control is another difficult aspect of living with this disorder. Children with asthma must remember to take medication daily or even several times a day at specific times. They also have to make sure their medication is with them at all times, just in case. This can be an extra challenge for children in split households, who do not have consistent oversight from one parent and therefore have to take more responsibility for their own health than other children of the same age. "Because my parents are divorced, it's very important to make sure I have my medicine at both houses,"[38] explains Alexis, a twelve-year-old girl with moderate asthma.

For children with severe asthma, medication may not be enough. These children may have to use special devices to test their lung function, sometimes several times a day. They decide what activities they can handle based on the results. Amy Van Dyken, who is an Olympic gold medal–winning swimmer, remembers having to do this as a teen. "I got a [device] to measure lung capacity," she says. "If I was in the green, I'd go all out and do a normal swim practice. If I was in the yellow, I'd warm up slowly, then see if it was green. If it was still in the yellow, the workout would be less intense. If I got to the pool and was in the red, I wouldn't set foot in the water."[39]

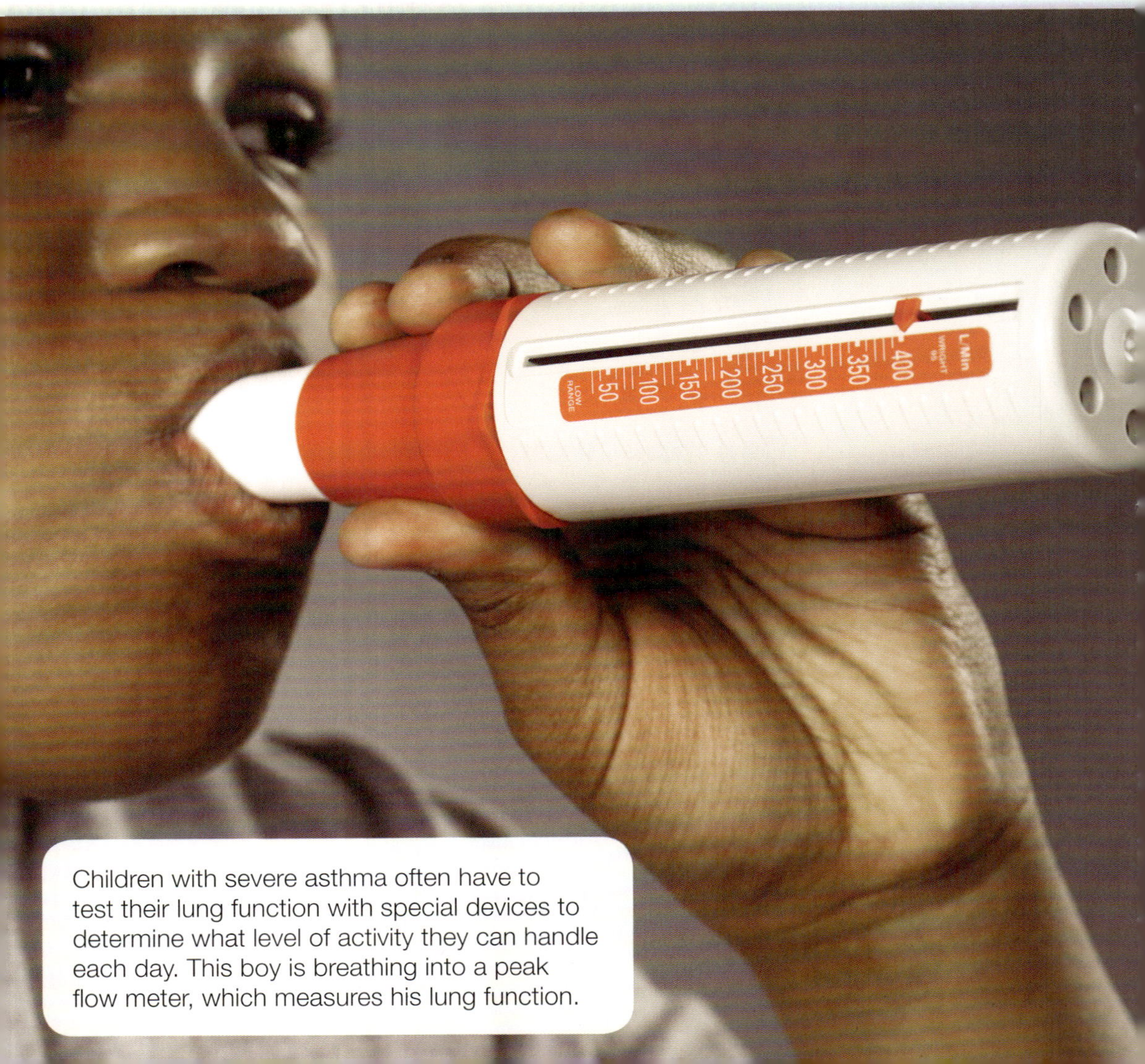

Children with severe asthma often have to test their lung function with special devices to determine what level of activity they can handle each day. This boy is breathing into a peak flow meter, which measures his lung function.

One young man has found an ingenious way to use his FitBit device to track his allergic responses. He sees when his heart is beating faster than usual, which is a sign of brewing allergies and the resulting asthma troubles. On an Internet message board, he explains how he headed off a health disaster on a recent trip. "My usual resting heart rate is about 59. I'm staying away from home for a few nights . . . [the] room looks clean. I sleep well through the night but wake up feeling tired. FitBit tells me my resting heart rate for that night was 77. So the next day I do my own deep clean [of the room] while wearing a mask. The next night I'm back to normal,"[40] he says. By monitoring his heart rate, this man was able to spot the signs of trouble and take action before his asthma could get out of control.

Social Stigma

Although constant monitoring is very helpful in managing asthma, it can be time-consuming and irritating. Making matters worse is the fact that children and young teenagers can be notoriously unaccepting of differences in others. They notice when one of their peers is coping with a chronic disorder such as asthma. They may shy away from that person, whom they perceive as being weird or different. They may even make rude comments to the asthmatic child about his or her symptoms, physical limitations, or other factors arising from asthma.

A 2012 study done in the UK tried to pinpoint the reasons behind this behavior. Called the "Room to Breathe" survey, it collected data from 943 families with asthmatic children. The survey found that reduced participation in sports and feelings of sadness were associated with increased bullying. Children with poor asthma control, too, were more likely to be targeted.

The good news is that these things can be changed. Most asthmatic children can participate in sports, with appropriate precautions, and they can get counseling to help with depression. They can also learn to control their asthma better. Still, the problem is real and kids do tease one another about perceived differences, including asthma. To avoid such teasing, many children and teens are reluctant to take necessary medicines for asthma in front of their peers or even to let others know when they do not feel well. This in turn can put them in danger of developing an asthma attack.

> **"One of the best ways to find relief from asthma symptoms is to learn about the illness."[42]**
>
> —WebMD

The good news is that teasing generally lets up with age. Older teens start to understand that everyone is different in some way, and they usually become more accepting of others. At the same time, teens who have health challenges usually become increasingly self-confident and less worried about what others think. "Sometimes I get teased about it. I just ignore them. It's usually only the idiots who haven't got the brains to think of anything else,"[41] says a student named Fran. In time any social stigma attached to asthma tends to fade away.

Taking Control

Growing older brings other positive changes for children with asthma. As the years pass, kids come to understand their bodies better and better. They know what symptoms they are likely to have, what generally triggers them, and how to avoid those triggers. They also know what to do when symptoms arise. They can tell when a simple puff of medicine will solve the problem, when stronger medications are needed—and most importantly, when to ask for help.

This level of knowledge is a big confidence booster. As popular medical website WebMD puts it:

> One of the best ways to find relief from asthma symptoms is to learn about the illness. A good understanding of your disease can ease the fear, the feeling of not knowing what's coming, and the anxiety around not being able to breathe freely. . . . When you pay attention to your body

and your surroundings, you're less likely to be surprised by a sudden attack. And you'll have peace of mind knowing how to handle one when it happens.[42]

Michael Rich, a pediatrician at Boston Children's Hospital, agrees. He strongly believes that asthma patients—even children—must be taught and empowered to take charge of their disorder. "The reality is that doctors aren't going to manage asthma," he says. "It's the people who have it who have to manage it. . . . It's not just about medicating a pair of lungs. It's about respecting your patients' lives and getting them to believe that they can take care of themselves."[43] When children develop the confidence to do this, everyone wins—families, doctors, and most importantly, the patients themselves.

A Healthy, Happy Life

A can-do attitude, unfortunately, cannot solve all health problems. Some children with asthma face a lifetime of medical struggles. They may even be permanently disabled by their condition, meaning that they are unable to work or hold down a job when they become adults. According to the World Health Organization, asthma is the fourteenth leading cause of disability worldwide.

> **"Most of the time I forget that I even have asthma, and I feel like all my other friends."[44]**
>
> —Alexis, asthma sufferer

Despite these frightening numbers, the outlook is good for most children with asthma, especially in developed countries where good health care is generally available. Alexis's experience is typical among this group. "Most of the time I forget that I even have asthma, and I feel like all my other friends," she says. "I would say to someone who is just finding out they had asthma that you can still do the activities you like and stuff, as long as you just listen to your doctor and take your medicine. So you can still be yourself."[44] With proper management, most youth—like Alexis—discover that living with asthma is not so bad after all.

Chapter 4

Can Asthma Be Treated or Cured?

Claire McCarthy is a doctor. She is also the parent of a child with asthma, and she vividly remembers how helpless her son's condition once made her feel. "My older son had asthma and would cough and have trouble breathing when he exercised. I worried about him every time he went to swim practice in elementary and middle school," she remembers. "[I] so wished there was something I could do to make the problem go away."[45]

McCarthy is not alone in feeling this way. Most parents wish they could wave a magic wand and make their child's asthma disappear. Many people who suffer from asthma have the same wish. They would like nothing more than to be cured and live a normal, asthma-free life.

Unfortunately for these people, no miracle cure currently exists. Once asthma sets in, it is considered to be chronic and incurable. A few decades ago, this condition had a major and ongoing impact on sufferers' lives. "People who had asthma accepted that they would just have a compromised life, both emotionally and physically,"[46] says Beth Eve Corn, medical director of the Division of Immunology Faculty Practice Associates at Mount Sinai Hospital in New York City.

Today, however, the situation has changed. Although asthma cannot be cured, it can now be controlled and managed very successfully through a combination of monitoring, medications, and simple lifestyle alterations. Ongoing research is also uncovering many exciting new avenues of exploration that are likely to improve the situation even further. Because of these factors, says Corn, "we [now] look at asthma very differently. Every asthmatic should be able to exercise, and every asthmatic should be under control and leading a normal life."[47]

> **"Every asthmatic should be able to exercise, and every asthmatic should be under control and leading a normal life."[47]**
>
> —Beth Eve Corn, medical director at Mount Sinai Hospital

A Correct Diagnosis

Diagnosing asthma is the first step in managing it. The child's doctor will do a careful physical examination and listen to the lungs and airways. The doctor will also check for a runny nose, sore throat, and other symptoms of the common cold. He or she may also order a chest X-ray to get a better look at the patient's lungs.

During the initial exam, the doctor will also ask the patient many questions to get a clear picture of his or her symptoms. The doctor will want to know if the symptoms appeared suddenly and recently or have been going on for a long time. He or she will ask if the symptoms get worse after exposure to certain substances or after certain activities. The doctor will also want to know about any allergies the patient may have, since allergies are closely linked to asthma, and will also ask about any family history of asthma.

If the patient's answers lead the doctor to suspect asthma, further tests may be ordered. A basic lung function exam called a spirometry test is usually the first step. In a spirometry test, patients blow as hard as they can into a tube that is connected to

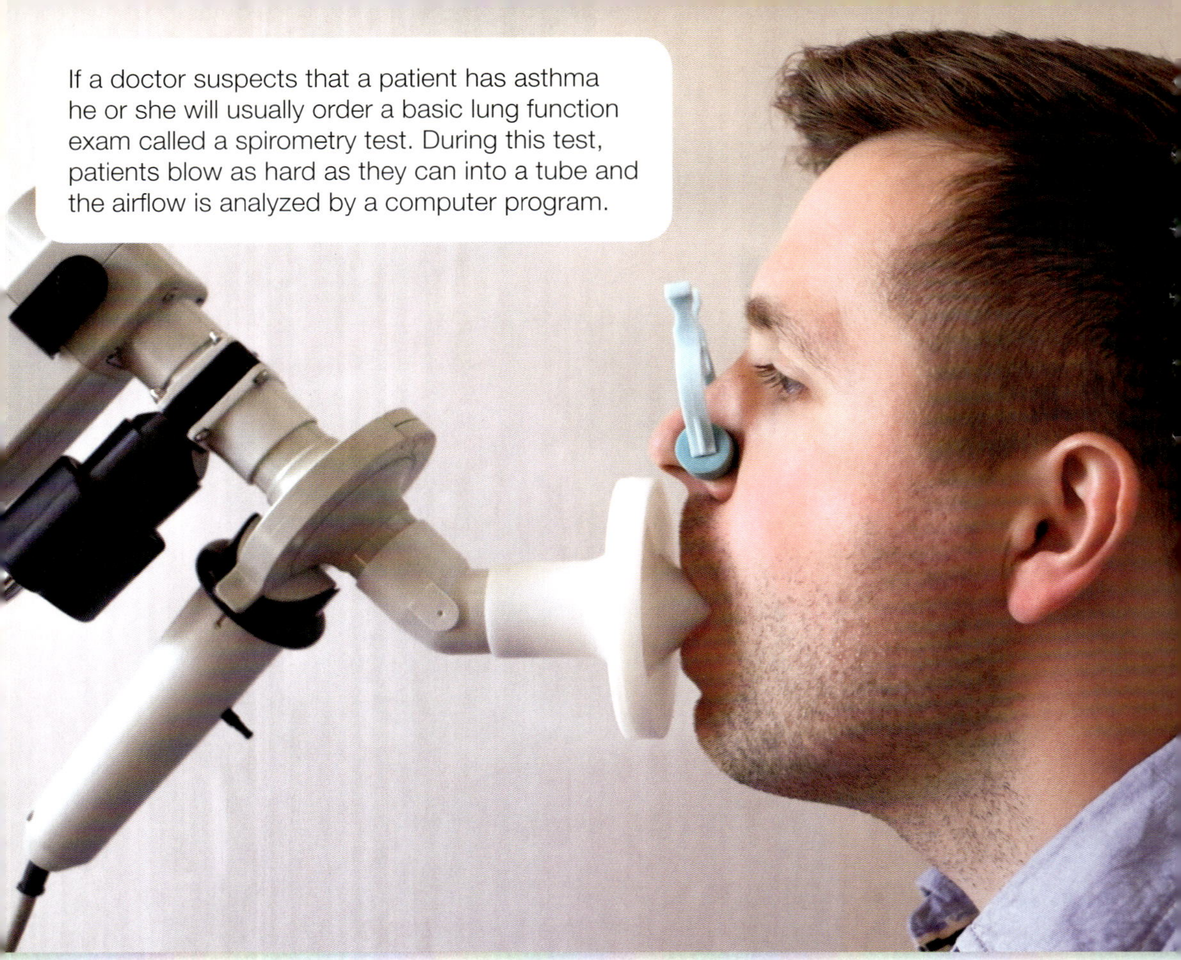

If a doctor suspects that a patient has asthma he or she will usually order a basic lung function exam called a spirometry test. During this test, patients blow as hard as they can into a tube and the airflow is analyzed by a computer program.

a computer. The computer analyzes the airflow to see if it is typical. If the airflow is lower than normal, the patient will be asked to inhale a medicine called a bronchodilator. This type of medicine very quickly reduces swelling and opens inflamed airways. After breathing the bronchodilator, the patient blows into the tube again. If the results show a significant improvement in lung function, it is very likely that the patient has asthma.

A different kind of test called a bronchoprovocation test works in exactly the opposite way: It provokes asthma symptoms instead of easing them. This test is used when asthma is suspected but the patient is not currently having any symptoms. First the patient does a spirometry test to measure lung capacity. Then the patient breathes in a small amount of medicine called methacholine. This medicine has little effect on patients without asthma. In asthmatic patients, however, methacholine irritates the airways and makes them constrict. By repeatedly measuring lung function during the test, doctors can determine if patients are asthmatic and, if so, how severe their condition is likely to be.

Two Types of Inhalers

Once a child has been diagnosed with asthma, medications will be prescribed to control his or her symptoms. Devices called inhalers are the most common form of asthma medication. These are L-shaped plastic tubes. A vial of medicine is inserted into the top part of the tube, and the lower part goes into the mouth. The vial is pressed downward to release a puff of medicine-laden vapor, which is then breathed deeply into the lungs.

Inhalers deliver two different types of medicine, and both are important. Preventer medication is steroid-based. It coats the insides of the airways like an invisible suit of armor, soothing irritated passageways and stopping them from swelling and becoming inflamed. This protective effect builds up over time. By taking the prescribed number of puffs each day, many patients can control their asthma so they never have attacks.

The second type of medication, known as rescue or reliever medicine, is delivered in the same way. Rescue medication is a fast-acting bronchodilator. This means it quickly reduces inflammation and swelling to ease asthma symptoms almost instantly. Rescue inhalers should be carried at all times and are used on an as-needed basis. The patient can take a puff several times a day or even several times in a row, if necessary, to reduce uncomfortable asthma symptoms.

It is very common for asthma patients, especially children, to use inhalers incorrectly. They do not feel any different after using their preventer inhaler, so they skip it. They depend on the rescue inhaler, which has an immediate and powerful effect—but which does nothing for the underlying problem. "Patients feel better after using a reliever inhaler, but they don't understand they are not 'treating' their asthma. The only way to control it is to use inhaled steroids (preventers) to reduce the inflammation that causes it,"[48] explains respiratory pharmacist Anna Murphy.

Spacers and Nebulizers

Inhalers of any type are not effective if the medicine they contain does not make it into the lungs. It can be tricky or impossible for some people, especially young children and babies, to master the technique of simultaneously pressing and inhaling. Also, for those with severe asthma or who are in the midst of an asthma attack, constricted airways can make it impossible to inhale quickly. Devices that simplify the process can be a big help for anyone who falls into these groups.

> **"Patients feel better after using a reliever inhaler, but they don't understand they are not 'treating' their asthma. The only way to control it is to use inhaled steroids."[48]**
>
> —Anna Murphy, respiratory pharmacist

One such device is called a spacer. Spacers are small chambers that attach to the breathing end of an inhaler. The other end is open and goes into the user's mouth. When the medicine vial is pressed, the mist enters the spacer. The user can then inhale the mist slowly, rather than having to suck it in with one giant gulp.

For those who cannot manage even a spacer, machines called nebulizers are a good option. The user wears a plastic breathing mask that may completely cover the nose and mouth, or may just have a mouthpiece. The mask is attached to a tube, which is attached to an electrical pump. Liquid medicine is put into a receptacle at the bottom of the mask. The pump forces air through the liquid and turns it into mist while the user breathes normally. It usually takes about fifteen minutes for a nebulizer to deliver a full dose of medicine—much longer than an inhaler, but effective and reliable for babies, toddlers, and anyone else who cannot manage a different treatment.

The Future of Asthma Treatment

Asthma treatment and prevention options have improved dramatically in recent decades. However, scientists continue to look for new strategies and medications that might improve the situation even further. Promising avenues of research include the following:

Monoclonal antibodies: Approved for human injection in 2015, these drugs reduce severe asthma attacks by cutting the levels of blood eosinophils, a type of white blood cell that contributes to the development of asthma.

Allergy immunotherapies: Certain drugs that boost the immune system can improve allergic responses or even cure them. This in turn may lead to reduced asthma symptoms.

Longer-acting bronchodilators: These medications will be delivered through inhalers like rescue and prevention medications are, but they will have a longer protective effect.

Antibiotics: A 2017 study showed that the common antibiotic azithromycin, taken three times per week, led to a 40 percent reduction in severe attacks among patients with persistent uncontrolled asthma.

Better screening and prevention: Early screening and prevention tools may be the best tool of all. By understanding which infants are at risk of developing asthma, doctors can take early and aggressive steps to keep them safe until their systems mature.

Many parents dread the prospect of trying to get their infants and active toddlers to sit still and tolerate a nebulizer treatment. Indeed, many children do resist this type of treatment at first. But as physician William E. Berger points out, "Even the smallest infants ultimately learn that nebulizer treatments make them feel better. Eventually, that realization makes the time you spend administering nebulizer therapy more effective, comfortable, and rewarding for both you and your child."[49]

Stepping It Up . . . and Down

While inhaled preventer and rescue medications are the first line of asthma treatment, they are not the only medications available. Some people with severe asthma require more aggressive treatment. They may take pills that reduce inflammation throughout the body or block it from occurring in the first place. They may also use long-lasting inhalers that work in a way similar to rescue inhalers but contain medicine that is slower to take effect and that continues working for twelve hours or more.

> **"Do not assume that you can decrease your dosage or stop taking a medication simply because you do not have symptoms. . . . Talk to your doctor if you think your medications should be altered."[50]**
>
> —American Academy of Allergy, Asthma & Immunology

In all asthma treatment, the goal is to take a stepwise approach. This means that the dosage and type of medicine used to control a person's asthma is carefully monitored and "stepped up" or "stepped down" as needed. When symptoms appear or increase, a doctor steps up the patient's medication little by little until the symptoms disappear. When a patient has been stable for a long time, the doctor may step the medication down. By experimenting with various combinations and amounts of medication, the doctor finds the right level to control the person's symptoms.

Patients may be tempted to ease off their medications when they have been symptom-free and feeling well for a long time. They might think they are better and do not need to keep up with a daily regimen. But doctors emphasize the importance of sticking to the plan. "Do not assume that you can decrease your dosage or stop taking a medication simply because you do not have symptoms. The purpose of the medication is to help you remain symptom-free. Talk to your doctor if you think your medications should be altered,"[50] warns the American Academy of Allergy, Asthma & Immunology.

Allergy Treatment

For children whose asthma is strongly related to allergies, medical treatment of the allergies may be necessary. When the allergies are well controlled, asthma symptoms will be greatly reduced or may disappear altogether.

The first step in treating allergies is determining exactly what allergens are giving the child trouble. To do this, doctors may order blood tests that measure the amount of an antibody called IgE in the bloodstream. They will do this test when the child's asthma symptoms are at their worst. They may also order a special test in which allergens are added directly to a sample of the child's blood. A technician watches the process through a microscope to see if a reaction occurs.

Skin prick tests provide another helpful piece of information. In these tests, a numbered grid is drawn on the skin of a child's arm or back. A technician then injects tiny amounts of allergens

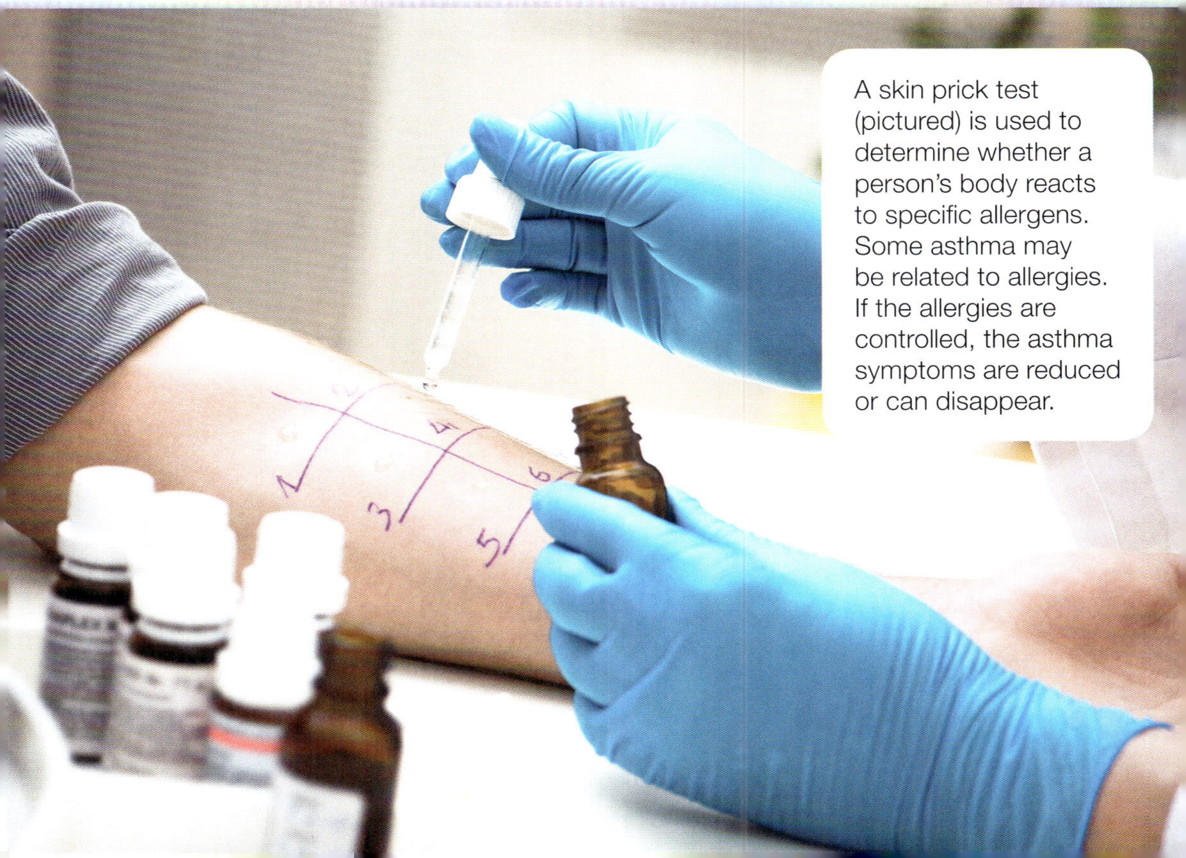

A skin prick test (pictured) is used to determine whether a person's body reacts to specific allergens. Some asthma may be related to allergies. If the allergies are controlled, the asthma symptoms are reduced or can disappear.

into each segment of the grid—a different allergen for each segment. The patient is then monitored to see which grids develop reactions, such as redness, swelling, or hives. The more strongly and quickly a segment reacts, the more severe the child's allergy to that particular allergen.

Once a doctor determines which allergens are a problem for the child, he or she may order a desensitization treatment. This is also called immunotherapy. In this procedure, technicians mix up a special cocktail containing minute amounts of the child's troublesome allergens. Because no two children are exactly alike, the mixtures must be carefully created for each individual. The child returns to the doctor's office once or twice a week for several

Can Kids Outgrow Asthma?

There is a common perception that children can outgrow asthma. It is true that some children become less symptomatic or even symptom-free with age. Scientists believe, however, that people with asthma are never truly cured. They may go into remission for years, decades, or even a lifetime—but the underlying symptoms are still there. They are just too minor to be noticed or to cause a problem.

There are many reasons asthma might seem to disappear as a child gets older. Physical growth is one factor. As a child's body gets bigger, the airways widen, and the lungs increase in size. Even if the airways are still somewhat irritated and inflamed, they are open enough to let air through, so the person does not notice any asthma symptoms.

Misdiagnosis is another possible reason. Many babies, toddlers, and young children wheeze and cough for reasons not related to asthma. It is not always easy for doctors to pinpoint the exact cause of these symptoms. If a doctor incorrectly assumes that asthma is at fault, the child may receive an asthma diagnosis and treatment—but the symptoms will disappear when the true issue goes away.

Although some asthmatic children get better with age, many do not. Recent studies have shown that children who are sensitive to allergens from a young age tend not to improve. Children with a skin disorder called eczema or a family history of asthma are also more likely to have lasting symptoms. For these children, "outgrowing" asthma—whatever the underlying medical reality—will probably never occur.

months to get injections of the mixture. The quantities of injected allergens are so tiny that the child's body can cope with them. Over time, the immune system learns to handle substances that previously caused a severe allergic reaction.

Immunotherapy is a major investment of time and money, since it may continue for many years. But people who see significant improvements in their allergy symptoms say it is worthwhile. "It's a long commitment and expense but it's been worth it to me. With the asthma and the amount of allergens I have, the shots have made a great improvement in my life,"[51] says one woman who is thrilled with her results.

Reducing Allergens

For those who do not or cannot undergo immunotherapy, lifestyle changes that reduce allergens may be effective. Reducing the impact of dust mites is a fairly easy step to take. Tight-woven bedcovers and pillowcases make it impossible for dust mites to get into mattresses and pillows. Frequent hot-water laundering of all bedding also helps. Carpets and drapes can be vacuumed regularly using vacuums equipped with HEPA (high-efficiency particle arrester) filters, which trap tiny particles, including dust mites. Some people with asthma find that they do better if they get rid of carpets and drapes altogether.

Cleaning products, tobacco smoke, and pet dander are other major indoor allergens. Depending on the individual, any or all of these problems may need to be addressed. Environmentally friendly or "green" cleaning products can be very helpful in reducing indoor fumes. Smoking indoors by parents or others can be avoided, or smoking can be stopped altogether. Pets can also be removed, although this is a heartbreaking step that most families are reluctant to take. If the child's allergies are not too severe, pets can sometimes be accommodated if they are kept in restricted areas or bathed frequently. Sometimes, however, pet allergies simply cannot be overcome. "It is so horrible to give little fur babies away but what can you do when people living in the house are suffering serious health consequences?"[52] asks one asthma sufferer who is struggling with pet issues.

Outdoor allergens are harder to control. Still, there are steps people with asthma can take to avoid major health problems. They can keep track of pollen counts and stay indoors on days when allergic triggers are most likely. For those who live in urban areas where pollution levels rise and fall, it might be necessary to stay inside on particularly bad days. These lifestyle changes and others can help people with asthma, of any age, manage their symptoms.

Natural Treatment

In recent years there has been a trend of people seeking nonmedical treatment for practically every health condition, and asthma is no exception. Adults and children alike are exploring many nonmedical ways to control their asthma symptoms.

Because asthma is a respiratory disorder, it is no surprise that many such treatments focus on breathing. Some asthmatics claim to benefit from yoga, which teaches breathing and relaxation techniques, among other things. Breath control helps with the moment-to-moment challenges of getting air into the system, while relaxation techniques are useful in managing the panic associated with asthma attacks. Another breathing technique called the Buteyko method emphasizes breathing through the nose to warm incoming air and protect the airways.

Acupuncture and massage are other popular treatments for asthma. In acupuncture, thin needles are inserted into the skin, targeting certain energy points that are thought to affect the entire body. Massage is more of a deep-muscle manipulation that promotes relaxation. Many people with asthma claim that one or both of these therapies give them symptom relief.

Vitamins and other supplements may also be part of an individual's asthma-relief regimen. There is some evidence that sup-

Some asthmatics say they benefit from yoga and its deep breathing and relaxation techniques. Breath control helps with moment-to-moment challenges of getting air into the system.

plements such as vitamin C, vitamin E, selenium, magnesium, and omega-3 fatty acids may help reduce asthma symptoms. Whatever evidence exists, however, is not strongly supported by scientific studies. For this reason, explains the organization Asthma UK, dietary supplements and other nonmedical asthma management approaches "are usually referred to as complementary therapies, not alternative therapies. This is because it's always best to use them alongside (to complement) your prescribed medicines, not instead of them (as an alternative)."[53] In other words, when it comes to controlling asthma, medically approved interventions are the only recommended approach.

Monitoring Asthma

Whatever medications or treatments a person with asthma uses, and no matter how successful they may be, careful monitoring is an essential part of any asthma management plan. Asthma symptoms can be minor enough to go unnoticed. If left unchecked, they can develop into a bigger problem. By paying close attention, a person can detect and treat an asthma flare-up in its earliest stages, before it can lead to a dangerous attack.

A device called a peak flow meter is an important part of the monitoring process. Peak flow meters are handheld devices with an open tube on one end and a measuring scale on the other end. A person blows as hard as possible into the tube. The air pressure moves a gauge on the scale to indicate the person's lung function. If the gauge falls into a safe range, called the green zone, lung function is normal. If it falls into a range called the yellow zone, this indicates reduced lung function. If the gauge drops into a range called the red zone, the individual's lung function is significantly reduced. An asthma attack is either imminent or already occurring.

Peak flow meters are very easy to use and can be managed by children as young as age five. They are usually used in the morning and at night, although people can use a peak flow meter anytime they want to check their lung function. Athletes, for example, may blow into their peak flow meter before a competition to see if they need a puff on their rescue inhaler.

Some people find it helpful to chart their peak flow results. A peak flow chart can reveal trends that occur over time and show if a person is steadily improving or getting worse. It can also help people become aware of things that consistently affect their breathing. If, for instance, a peak flow chart reveals that a child's lung function is always a little low on Tuesday nights, and Tuesday is soccer night, it is likely that physical activity is triggering asthma symptoms.

Along with peak flow monitoring, a person with asthma should also track his or her rescue inhaler usage and symptoms in an asthma diary. This information should be reviewed at regular medical checkups so the individual's doctor can prescribe the right course of treatment.

Creating an Asthma Action Plan

In between doctor visits, a written asthma action plan can be a big help in managing asthma. An asthma plan is a highly individualized tool, developed by each patient together with his or her medical team. It lists a patient's known asthma triggers and allergies, along with medications, dosages, and instructions. It includes a detailed explanation of exactly what to do under different circumstances—for example, if the patient feels breathless or wheezy or cannot stop coughing. It also includes a list of emergency contact numbers in case assistance is needed for a severe asthma attack.

Although an asthma action plan is mostly a self-management tool, it is important for other key people to have copies and to be aware of the information it contains. For children, the circle of key people includes parents, babysitters or other caretakers, school nurses and possibly teachers, sports coaches, and anyone else who regularly interacts with the child without a parent present. All of these people need to know what to do if a dangerous situation arises.

"We are making progress—but health care providers, parents, caregivers, and schools can do more to help children avoid asthma attacks."[54]

—Anne Schuchat, acting director of the CDC

Studies show that asthma plans do improve outcomes for children with asthma. According to one recent US study, however, less than half of the children surveyed had such a plan. Although this study evaluated a limited area, its results are likely consistent across the United States. "We are making progress—but health care providers, parents, caregivers, and schools can do more to help children avoid asthma attacks,"[54] said Dr. Anne Schuchat of the CDC in a news release about the report.

Staying Well

The medical community agrees that where asthma is concerned, knowledge is the key to success. Patients must be educated about their symptoms and treatment and understand how to manage their condition. Doctors must take the time to hear, understand, and address each patient's individual concerns. And in the case of asthmatic children, parents must be involved and vigilant. Says physician Pat Bass:

> It's important not to grasp at signs of improvement as evidence of a turnaround. Work with your doctor and keep monitoring your child's condition as a matter of course. That includes annual flu vaccinations, regular doctor visits, and the avoidance of any asthma triggers in your everyday life.
>
> By doing so, you'll be better prepared to deal [with] a severe attack if one occurs and will instinctively know when it's time to act and seek emergency care.[55]

This type of constant vigilance can be difficult and stressful, but it is effective. When asthma is carefully monitored and its symptoms addressed, it is easier to control. With care and education, kids with asthma—and their families—can have every expectation of good health.

Source Notes

Introduction: The Most Common Chronic Disease of Youth

1. Neel Duggal, "What Does It Feel like to Live with Asthma?," Healthline, June 17, 2016. www.healthline.com.
2. Duggal, "What Does It Feel like to Live with Asthma?"
3. Quoted in Yella Hewings-Martin, "Asthma: Redefining This Silent Killer," Medical News Today, September 27, 2017. www.medicalnewstoday.com.

Chapter 1: What Is Asthma?

4. angelbaby3_02, comment on Carrcakes, "How Do Your Kids Describe Asthma Symptoms?," BabyCenter Community, February 13, 2010. www.community.babycenter.com.
5. brett'smom59, comment on Carrcakes, "How Do Your Kids Describe Asthma Symptoms?"
6. 5parker family, comment on Carrcakes, "How Do Your Kids Describe Asthma Symptoms?"
7. Quoted in Healthtalk.org, "What Asthma Feels Like," 2018. www.healthtalk.org.
8. Quoted in Healthtalk.org, "What Asthma Feels Like."
9. Partners Asthma Center, "What Is Meant by 'Inflammation' in Asthma?," 2010. www.asthma.partners.org.
10. Mehmet Oz, "What Does an Asthma Attack Feel Like?," Sharecare. www.sharecare.com.
11. Michelle Andrews, "What an Asthma Attack Feels like, for Those Who Have Never Had One," Mamamia, February 18, 2017. www.mamamia.com.au.

12. Quoted in David S. Martin, "Are Schools Making Kids Sick?," CNN, January 14, 2012. www.cnn.com.
13. Anna Feldweg, "How Do Adults Suddenly Get Asthma?," Everyday Health, April 16, 2007. www.everydayhealth.com.
14. Pat Bass, "The Risk of a Fatal Asthma Attack," Verywell Health, December 19, 2017. www.verywell.com.

Chapter 2: What Causes Asthma?

15. MLNewkirk, comment on Asthma Boards, "Do Your Parents or Siblings Suffer from Asthma?," 2018. www.asthmaboards.com.
16. kerin65, comment on Asthma Boards, "Do Your Parents or Siblings Suffer from Asthma?"
17. Gelsemium, comment on Asthma Boards, "Do Your Parents or Siblings Suffer from Asthma?"
18. Partners Asthma Center, "Chapter 34: Is Asthma Inherited?," 2010. www.asthma.partners.org.
19. Ari Brown and Denise Fields, *Baby 411: Clear Answers and Smart Advice for Your Baby's First Year*. Boulder, CO: Windsor Peak, 2017.
20. Kenzie, comment on Cook, "The Allergy Triad: Allergies-Eczema-Asthma," Willing Cook, June 27, 2011. https://willingcook.com.
21. Quoted in SampleSize, "Help for Cat-Induced Asthma?," Ask MetaFilter, August 6, 2009. https://ask.metafilter.com.
22. Quoted in Centers for Disease Control and Prevention, "Asthma and Secondhand Smoke," January 23, 2017. www.cdc.gov.
23. 5hep06, comment on TiberiumBoss, "Not Sure If I Like Summer as I Don't Get a Cold, or Whether I Like Winter as I Don't Get Hay Fever!," Reddit, 2017. www.reddit.com.
24. Quoted in Rebecca Kolp, "Asthma During Pregnancy," Bump, 2018. www.thebump.com.

Chapter 3: What Is It like to Live with Ashtma?

25. John Bottrell, "Can You Really Live a Normal Life with Asthma?," HealthCentral, October 1, 2012. www.healthcentral.com.

26. Bottrell, “Can You Really Live a Normal Life with Asthma?”
27. Nicole, personal communication, February 26, 2018.
28. Quoted in Healthtalk.org, “What Asthma Feels Like.”
29. Theresa Cannizzaro, “What Does an Asthma Attack Feel Like?,” Asthma.net, September 20, 2016. https://asthma.net.
30. Andrews, “What an Asthma Attack Feels like, for Those Who Have Never Had One.”
31. Vann R. Newkirk II, “How to Beat Asthma,” *Atlantic*, July 5, 2017. www.theatlantic.com.
32. Quoted in Healthtalk.org, “Childhood Onset,” 2018. www.healthtalk.org.
33. Kat, “Kat’s Asthma Story,” KidsHealth. https://kidshealth.org.
34. Kat, “Kat’s Asthma Story.”
35. Quoted in Healthtalk.org, “Changing Symptoms Over Time,” 2018. www.healthtalk.org.
36. 399611, comment on toxicsword, “How Do You Live with Asthma Allergy?,” Reddit, 2018. www.reddit.com.
37. moutankal, “Depressed from Asthma,” Reddit, February 27, 2018. www.reddit.com.
38. Alexis, “Asthma: Alexis’ Story,” KidsHealth. https://kidshealth.org.
39. Quoted in Anne Stein, “Interview: Breathless in Sydney,” HealthDay, January 20, 2018. https://consumer.healthday.com.
40. archali, comment on mgwilliams11, “I Want to Get to Know What It’s like to Have Asthma (Or to Take Care of an Asthmatic Person),” Reddit, 2017. www.reddit.com.
41. Quoted in Sarah Lennard-Brown, *Asthma*. Austin, TX: Raintree Steck-Vaughn, 2003, p. 59.
42. WebMD, “Asthma Relief and Natural Remedies,” May 10, 2017. www.webmd.com.
43. Quoted in Sara Corbett, “The Asthma Trap,” *Mother Jones*, March/April 2005. www.motherjones.com.
44. Alexis, “Asthma.”

Chapter 4: Can Asthma Be Treated or Cured?

45. Claire McCarthy, “How to Manage Your Child’s Asthma,” *Parents*, May 2013. www.parents.com.
46. Quoted in Sanjay Gupta, “What Is Allergic Asthma, and What Can I Do About It?,” Everyday Health, March 14, 2016. www.everydayhealth.com.

47. Quoted in Gupta, "What Is Allergic Asthma, and What Can I Do About It?"
48. Quoted in Helen Wright, "How an Error Made by So Many Asthma Patients Left Terrified Helen Gasping for Air: Sufferers Don't Understand Preventer Inhalers or Forget to Use Them," *Daily Mail* (London), August 17, 2015. www.dailymail.co.uk.
49. William E. Berger, *Allergies and Asthma for Dummies*. Foster City, CA: IDG Books Worldwide, 2000, p. 239.
50. American Academy of Allergy, Asthma & Immunology, "Follow the Stepwise Approach for Asthma Control," 2018. www.aaaai.org.
51. oally, comment on undsoft, "Did Anyone Have Allergen Immunotherapy?," Reddit, 2017. www.reddit.com.
52. SeriousDogProbs, "Help! Allergies and Asthma and Pets—Long Story," Reddit, 2017. www.reddit.com.
53. Asthma UK, "Complementary Therapies," March 2017. www.asthma.org.uk.
54. Quoted in Susan Perry, "Childhood Asthma Rates Are Declining, but Disparities Persist," *MinnPost*, February 12, 2018. www.minnpost.com.
55. Pat Bass, "Is My Child at Risk of a Fatal Asthma Attack?," Verywell Health, October 31, 2017. www.verywell.com.

Organizations and Websites

Allergy and Asthma Foundation of America (AAFA)
8201 Corporate Dr., Suite 1000
Landover, MD 20785
www.aafa.org

The AAFA is the world's oldest asthma and allergy patient group. The organization's website has information on asthma and allergy programs, research, advocacy, events, and more.

Allergy & Asthma Network
8229 Boone Blvd., Suite 260
Vienna, VA 22182
www.asthmaallergynetwork.org

The Allergy & Asthma Network is the leading nonprofit patient education and advocacy organization for people with asthma, allergies, and related conditions. Its website makes accurate medical information relevant and understandable to all while promoting evidence-based standards of care.

American Academy of Allergy, Asthma & Immunology
555 E. Wells St., Suite 1100
Milwaukee, WI 53202
www.aaaai.org

This site includes information on all aspects of asthma and allergies. It includes a kids' section with games and age-appropriate resources.

American College of Allergy, Asthma & Immunology

85 W. Algonquin Rd., Suite 550
Arlington Heights, IL 60005
https://acaai.org

This organization offers an authoritative, well-organized website that covers all the basics of asthma and allergies.

American Lung Association

55 W. Wacker Dr., Suite 1150
Chicago, IL 60601
www.lung.org

The American Lung Association works to save lives by improving lung health and preventing lung disease through research, education, and advocacy. Its website provides information on all major lung diseases, including asthma.

Centers for Disease Control and Prevention (CDC)

1600 Clifton Rd.
Atlanta, GA 30329
www.cdc.gov

The CDC is America's most authoritative organization on diseases and disorders. Its website offers a wealth of information about all major health challenges, including asthma.

For Further Research

Books

Sarah Brewer, *Overcoming Asthma: The Complete Complementary Health Program*. London: Watkins, 2014.

Leo Galland and Jonathan Galland, *The Allergy Solution: Unlock the Surprising, Hidden Truth About Why You Are Sick and How to Get Well*. Carlsbad, CA: Hay House, 2016.

Fiona Heggie and Ellie Lux, *The Allergy-Free Family Cookbook: 100 Delicious Recipes Free from Dairy, Eggs, Peanuts, Tree Nuts, Soya, Gluten, Sesame and Shellfish*. London: Orion, 2015.

Amy Myers, *The Autoimmune Solution: Prevent and Reverse the Full Spectrum of Inflammatory Symptoms and Diseases*. New York: HarperCollins, 2015.

Sasha Yakovleva et al., *Breathe to Heal: Break Free from Asthma*. Lyons, CO: Breathing Center, 2016.

Internet Sources

Michelle Andrews, "What an Asthma Attack Feels like, for Those Who Have Never Had One," Mamamia, February 18, 2017. www.mamamia.com.au/what-does-an-asthma-attack-feel-like.

Neel Duggal, "What Does It Feel like to Live with Asthma?," Healthline, June 17, 2016. www.healthline.com/health/what-does-an-asthma-attack-feel-like.

David S. Martin, "Are Schools Making Kids Sick?," CNN, January 14, 2012. www.cnn.com/2012/01/14/health/school-indoor-air-pollution/index.html.

Emiliano Rodriguez Mega, "Are Pets Good or Bad for Your Child's Allergies?," *Scienceline*, January 31, 2018. https://scienceline.org.

Vann R. Newkirk II, "How to Beat Asthma," *Atlantic*, July 5, 2017. www.theatlantic.com.

Steven Reinberg, "Asthma Attacks on the Decline Among U.S. Kids," *U.S. News & World Report*, February 6, 2018. https://health.usnews.com.

Index

Note: Boldface page numbers indicate illustrations.

Picture Credits

Cover: Buenadventuramariano/iStockphoto.com

7: Maury Aaseng

11: Innerspace Imaging/Science Source

15: Anatomical Travelogue/Science Source

18: RyanJLane/iStockphoto.com

25: JGA/Shutterstock.com

31: Hannah Maule-Ffinch Image Source/Newscom

35: Dirima/Shutterstock.com

41: FatCamera/iStockphoto.com

44: Maury Aaseng

48: Coney/Jay/Science Source

54: Koldunova_Anna/iStockphoto.com

59: AlexRaths/iStockphoto.com

63: FatCamera/iStockphoto.com

About the Author

Kris Hirschmann has written more than four hundred books for children. She owns and runs a business that provides a variety of writing and editorial services. She lives just outside Orlando, Florida, with her daughters, Nikki and Erika.